✛✛✛✛✛✛✛✛✛✛✛✛✛✛✛✛✛✛✛✛✛✛✛✛✛✛✛✛✛✛✛✛✛✛✛✛✛✛

The Secret of
Belledonne Room 16

The Secret of Belledonne Room 16

by Anke de Vries

McGraw-Hill Book Company

New York   St. Louis   San Francisco

Library of Congress Cataloging in Publication Data

Vries, Anke de, 1936-
The secret of Belledonne room 16.
Translation of Belledonne kamer 16.
Summary: A few cryptic phrases in a notebook and a bul-
let found among his grandfather's effects in Paris after his
death start a 17-year-old on a quest that leads him to the
French Alps.
[1. Mystery and detective stories. 2. France—Fiction]
I. Title.
PZ7.V986Se [Fic] 79-12040
ISBN 0-07-020109-9

1 2 3 4 5 6 7 8 9 MUMU 7 8 3 2 1 0 9

++

The Secret of
Belledonne Room 16

++++++++++++++++++++++++++++++++++++++

chapter one

"You're not going, do you hear! You're not going!" the old woman shouted, angrily straightening her apron.

"But it's a funeral . . . ," the man interrupted.

"A funeral," she snorted. "A funeral . . . for others, maybe, but not for you. Oh, no! For you she isn't dead. And she won't ever be dead either. Even if she's lying, rotting fifty meters under the ground!"

"Ta gueule . . . hold your tongue." The man spoke softly, almost threateningly.

Robert hesitated. He'd already been standing in the doorway of the café for some time. Neither of the people had noticed him.

"And why should I have to hold my tongue?" the woman stormed. "I, your own wife?"

The man laughed scornfully. "You, you don't even know what a wife is."

Robert saw her profile; a nose that stuck out sharply, just as her chin did. The shutters of the café were half closed to keep out the heat, but he could imagine her grim mouth even in the dimness.

"You're the only one who knows that, eh?" she sneered. "You know only too well what a wife is. You've got experience, haven't you? Ha!" Her voice lashed out. "You've made a fool out of me. A complete fool. For years. Everyone in the village knows it. First with Florette, then that Mireille . . . "

"Don't start that again! *Bon dieu . . . .*" His voice sounded weary.

"I wouldn't be starting again if you hadn't."

The man shrugged his shoulders and leaned over the bar counter. He was unbelievably heavy.

"That didn't mean a thing," he sighed.

The woman laughed shrilly. "Monsieur claims it didn't mean a thing. Madame Girauld was the only one who meant anything, eh? But she's dead," she shrieked triumphantly. "Your beautiful Madame Girauld is dead. Stone dead. Gone!" As if that wasn't enough, she grabbed a bottle from the bar and banged it down wildly on the counter.

Robert felt he should act. That woman would soon be breaking the bottle over the fat man's head.

He moved back a pace nervously, but forgot about the two steps. His foot brushed past the stone. He lost his balance and fell.

"Is anyone there?"

The woman jerked around and shot to the doorway.

Robert scrambled to his feet and brushed the dust off his trousers.

"I tripped," he mumbled.

"You're not the first and probably not the last either to have that happen," the fat man remarked, visibly relieved at the interruption.

"I've always told you, you should do something about those rotten steps," the woman snapped before disappearing.

The man took Robert's arm. "Come inside, *mon garçon*, come inside. It's much too hot out. Not healthy for a normal person."

Robert picked up his duffel bag and followed him into the café.

"Do you want something to drink?"

"Yes, please. A Coke. I'm dying of thirst." The man poured a Coke out for himself too before sitting down at the table opposite Robert. The wooden chair was much too small for him.

"On vacation?" he asked, wiping the back of his hand across his mouth. Robert nodded and examined the man. His face was peculiar. Wide and full, with a few wrinkles. Thin, damp hair stuck to his head. It was the expression in his eyes that was particularly strange, Robert thought. A child's gaze, gentle and innocent. It was as if the eyes had been put into that head by accident.

"Are you camping around here?" the man inquired.

"No, I've just arrived and I'm looking for a room. The sign outside said 'La Taverne, M. and Mme. Alban Mons, proprietors.' You are Monsieur Mons?"

The man nodded.

"Is this a pension?" Robert's eyes swept the room.

"Was before. Not any longer. You might still get something below in the village, though ... it's high season. There's a hotel right by the main road."

Robert said nothing and took a gulp from his glass.

"Where are you from?" the older man asked.

"Holland."

"Holland? You're not French? You speak ...."

"My mother is French," Robert explained.

"Ah, that's why." Monsieur Mons grinned. "I'd already thought .... See," he went on when he saw Robert's questioning glance, "see, when you fell there, you didn't say anything. Up till now not one Frenchman has tumbled down those stairs without calling on a few saints."

He put his big hand on Robert's arm. "That would of course have been different if your father had been French, but your mother ... that's a woman. They aren't so quick to swear, although ...." Monsieur Mons was obviously thinking about his own wife, because he said: "All depends, of course. So you come from Holland," he went on. "Doctor Perrin went there once. To Amsterdam. He thought

4

the tulips were beautiful, but the coffee was undrinkable. Apparently you put a syrupy kind of milk in it."

Robert smiled. "Wasn't this café called Belledonne before?"

Robert's question came out carelessly, but he felt the hand resting on his leg clench tensely.

"Yes, indeed!" Monsieur Mons exclaimed, "but that's a long time ago, mind. You weren't even in the world then."

Robert drew a deep breath. He had found it! About a week's searching, but now he had finally found it!

"Why did it become 'La Taverne'?"

"Ah, why? I wouldn't know. Probably a woman behind it. You know how they are. Always changing names. If they're called Sophie, it has to be Marie, and if they're called Marie then one fine day they'll only answer to the name Claire. I think it was the same with Belledonne."

"It's just as beautiful a name."

"I agree with you. The mountain the other side of the valley is called that." Monsieur Mons produced a grimy handkerchief and wiped his neck and forehead with it.

"It was already called La Taverne when we bought it," he said. "At first we went on renting rooms because it had always been a pension. But the last few years we haven't done that any more. *La vieille,* the old woman, you understand ... she's a rotten type." Monsieur Mons nervously turned his head towards the door, from behind which a muffled clatter could be heard.

"But how did you come to know that this used to be called Belledonne?" he asked quickly, rather surprised.

Robert had expected the question. But his stomach knotted up now that it was asked.

"I had an . . . I had an uncle who came here."

It sounded perfectly normal.

"An uncle?"

"Yes. His name was Robert Macy."

The fat man wiped his forehead again and used the handkerchief to wave away the flies that had gathered in the rim of his glass. "Means nothing to me. Robert Macy . . . ." He repeated the name slowly. "When was he here?"

"Ages ago. At the end of the war."

"That could fit, because it became 'La Taverne' after the war. Did your uncle give you the address?"

Robert shook his head. His heart suddenly began to thump. "No, I've never seen him. He disappeared. The last thing we know of him is that he came here once."

Monsieur Mons shifted a bit. The chair creaked ominously.

"Is that why you've come—because your uncle visited this pension about thirty years ago? That's nice, that's nice. I wish someone would come here looking for me in thirty years' time . . . even if only to say: Alban Mons lived here. Nothing else . . . ." Monsieur Mons's gentle eyes grew somber, as if he already knew that would never happen.

"But it was empty at the end of the war!" he exclaimed suddenly. "Did you know that?"

"No."

"Well and truly empty. We took it over in 'forty-eight for a reasonable price because it was going badly. It was too

6

far from Nizier, the village, and there weren't any tourists in those days as there are now. People had to get over the war first, you see. The folks we bought it from had only kept it up for two years. Then they'd had enough. They must have bought it for peanuts because it had been empty for a time before that."

He glanced nervously at the door.

"I've sometimes thought that there's a curse on it. People stay away. It's never done well."

"Why not? The view's marvelous."

"Outside, yes," Monsieur Mons signed, "but it's different inside. *La vieille,* you see." He nodded almost imperceptibly towards the door.

"That old woman doesn't want any improvements. She's as tight as the plague. 'What's good for us is good enough for others,' she always says. But people won't put up any more with not being able to wash and so on. So we stopped renting rooms. She wouldn't have a young maid around, either. She can't bear the thought of having one near her—near me, then—" he corrected himself, "because she's stinking jealous."

He shook his heavy head resignedly.

"What do you think—might I be able to rent a room here just the same?" Robert persisted. "I'm really not demanding. It doesn't even matter if I have to sleep on the floor."

Monsieur Mons considered him. The tired creases in his face moved towards a grin.

"As far as I'm concerned, yes, always, *mon garçon.* If you'd been a girl you wouldn't have stood a chance, but I'll go and see what I can work out for you. I make no promises."

He pulled himself up, groaned, dabbed his forehead and neck with his handkerchief and puffed: "*Mon dieu,* how hot it is."

Robert waited tensely. The voices behind the door were muffled but he could hear from their tone that his request had set off more bickering. He glanced around the room. Would it have looked so bare and rundown thirty years ago? It certainly didn't look as if there'd been any renovations since. Only the tasteless plastic tablecloths on the wooden tables were recent.

He was startled when the door opened suddenly. Madame Mons appeared. Her hands restlessly fussed the blue-checked apron. Her feet were pushed into black sandals, above which a bare bit of leg was visible.

"Why do you want to rent a room?" The question was abrupt and suspicious.

"But I've already explained that to you," began Monsieur Mons weakly.

"I'm not asking you, I'm asking him." An angry finger pointed in Robert's direction.

"I'm on vacation, and, er . . . ." Robert tried cautiously.

"Are you on your own?" she interrupted.

"Yes, Madame."

"And tomorrow there'll be a visit from a girlfriend, eh?" The woman's split chin stuck out worse than ever.

"No, Madame, there's no girlfriend. I'm alone."

8

"That's what they all say," she commented scornfully. "Friends? Will friends be coming?"

"No friends either."

"But *nom de dieu,* you can surely see that he's alone?" Monsieur Mons cried.

"That doesn't mean a thing. Once he's here the rest'll come tomorrow. Then we might be overrun by hash smokers."

Monsieur Mons shrugged his shoulders despairingly.

"She saw a film on TV a year ago about lads who were smoking hash," he explained to Robert. "Now she believes that every fellow is walking around with a kilo of hash on him."

"I don't smoke hash," Robert told her quietly, "nor even cigarettes." She sized him up. Her eyes pierced through him, but he returned her gaze as calmly as he could.

"Bon, you can stay," she decided after a while. She stepped inside for a few minutes, then came back with some bed linen. "Here, my husband will show you a room."

She turned around abruptly and disappeared.

Robert followed Monsieur Mons up the stairs. It took a long time.

Everything gave an impression of poverty. The banisters were dilapidated, the yellowed paper was peeling away. The stairs were discolored and creaked.

"Wait a moment, I'm not twenty any longer," Monsieur

Mons gasped and stopped climbing. He closed his eyes. His chest heaved laboriously in and out. His light-green shirt was soaked. "I hardly ever come upstairs," he said a moment later. "We sleep downstairs. You can see why, of course." He pointed toward all the surplus weight he was carrying around.

"Don't ask me to bring you breakfast in bed," he said with a wry grin, "because that would chase me straight into my grave."

At the word "grave," his expression changed.

"Must ask you something in a moment," he whispered to Robert.

With a groan, he started off again.

"Monsieur," Robert said when they were finally upstairs, "could I possibly have room sixteen?"

"*Comment?* What did you say?"

"Room sixteen."

"Why?" Monsieur Mons turned round. His glance was suddenly suspicious.

"Sixteen is my lucky number," Robert improvised wildly. "When I buy a lottery ticket I always choose a number ending with sixteen. There are five rooms here next to each other, from ten to eighteen. They're all empty, after all, so I thought . . . ."

"You'll get room fourteen," Monsieur Mons retorted curtly. "It's just as big and the view is the same."

He already had the door open. The room was dark because the shutters were closed and it smelled stuffy. It must have been closed up tightly for months.

Monsieur Mons walked to the window. After some clumsy jerking, the windows gave in and flew open. The heat blasted in, smothering the room.

"We're certain to get a storm," Monsieur Mons predicted. "That'd be a relief. We've already had this weather for fourteen days. You can't get away from it. Do you think you can manage here?"

Robert looked around. There was a large bare wooden bed with a small cupboard next to it. A rickety table with a stoneware basin stood against the wall. A brown wardrobe took up most of the other wall.

"Fine," said Robert. "Except ... is there any water nearby?"

"There's a tap at the end of the passage. Just fill your basin with water when you want to wash." Monsieur Mons pointed to the stone basin. "Throw the water away down the lavatory. You'll find that along the passage."

"How much is the room a night?"

"You'll have to talk to *la vieille* about money. I don't get involved in it. Not that I get the chance to, anyway. How long do you think you'll stay?"

Robert shrugged. "I don't know yet, exactly."

Monsieur Mons grinned at him encouragingly. "I'll see if I can get a special price for you." His thumb pointed at the floor, under which, a few meters below them, Madame Mons was pottering about somewhere. Robert walked to the window and looked out. There was the wide valley with the mountains in the background, hazy in the heat. One of the mountains was called Belledonne .... How quiet it was here; a heavy, close quietness that was almost oppressive.

He heard Monsieur Mons cough behind him. When he turned around he saw the fat man staring down at his shoes in embarrassment. Slippers. Big wide slippers, Robert noticed. Of course, he probably couldn't even bend down to tie his shoelaces.

Monsieur Mons coughed again. "I have to ask you something. A favor. At least I've helped you to get this room. That wasn't so easy." The thumb pointed again at the floor.

"Of course," Robert said. "What can I do for you?"

"Attend a funeral tomorrow."

"Madame Girauld's funeral?" It was out before Robert realized it.

"Did you know her, then?" Monsieur Mons stammered with amazement.

"No, but, er . . . I happened to hear her name dropped when I arrived."

"Oh, yes, of course. You came in time, otherwise something else might have dropped besides her name," Monsieur Mons commented sourly.

"La vieille doesn't want me to go to the funeral. She's even jealous of the dead."

"What do I have to do?"

"Watch. Just watch. And tell me everything exactly as you see it. And then . . . ."

Monsieur Mons's face turned an alarming shade of purple. He rummaged nervously in his pocket and his hand came out with a ten-franc note. "Then buy a rose with this. One, mind. That won't be so noticeable among all the wreaths and bouquets. One rose isn't so expensive, either ...." He held out the ten francs before him, almost entreatingly.

Robert thought, His wife knows nothing about this.

"You'll be sure to choose the most beautiful, eh? You will do it, won't you?" The man's voice was pleading now. "You must choose the most beautiful of all. And not a red one. She didn't like red. Red is the color of blood, she once said to me. That's why it has to be yellow. A soft yellow, just like the dress she was wearing when I saw her last. Put that rose on her coffin when everyone has left. When you are alone with her. Then say . . . then you have to say: 'This is Alban Mons's rose. He is grateful to you for all your visits. He will never forget them ....'" His voice broke. *"Voilà, c'est tout.* That's all."

"Do you think you can remember that?" he almost stuttered.

It was the most unexpected and strangest favor Robert could have imagined. If he were ever to speak about this no one would believe him. A yellow rose for Madame Giraud's grave .... He suppressed a nervous inclination to laugh. Monsieur Mons's red face was dead earnest.

"You will do it for me, won't you, eh?"

"I'm quite happy to," Robert began carefully, "but won't it be peculiar for a complete stranger to be attending the funeral? I didn't even know her."

A crafty glitter appeared in the fat man's eyes.

"It doesn't have to be peculiar. Not at all. Because you, *mon garçon,* will be at the graveyard tomorrow quite by coincidence, looking for your Uncle Robert's grave. After all, he could be dead, couldn't he? You've got every right to be there, even if there's a funeral going on."

Robert nodded. Monsieur Mons was shrewder than he had thought.

"You can keep the change," he said when Robert took the note, "that's for your trouble. But not a word about this. Not to anyone. Otherwise—" Monsieur Mons looked at him, but then shrugged his shoulders, probably realizing that a threat wouldn't help.

"I shan't talk to anyone about it," Robert promised. "You can rely on that."

Monsieur Mons put his hand on Robert's shoulder. *"Merci, mon garçon. Merci."*

After that, he turned around and waddled to the door.

"You really know what you have to say, eh?" he asked before going out.

"I've got a good memory."

"And you'll pick out the most beautiful? The most beautiful of all?"

"I promise."

When the door closed at last, Robert walked over to the window again and took a deep breath.

God, how that man stank. It was a complete mystery to him how a man like that could have had a girlfriend. A girlfriend who was now dead and to whom he should take a yellow rose . . . incredible!

Still—Robert stared at the mountains and thought—it was no more of a mystery than Robert Macy.

His being in this rundown café that had once been a pension was all due, in fact, to a simple notebook. A notebook that was more than thirty years old and that had belonged to a certain Robert Macy.

He had told Monsieur Mons that Robert Macy was his uncle, but that was a lie. He hadn't the slightest clue who the man was!

✦✦

chapter two

Robert stretched dully. His mouth was dry and the sheets that Madame Mons had given him felt clammy from the heat. The storm hadn't broken in the night and it promised to be another sultry day. He slid out of bed and went to fill the stoneware bowl under the tap in the passage. It took a long time with the economically thin stream of water that trickled out.

Back in his room, he washed. Then he rubbed his chin. He could wait another day before shaving; he didn't have to shave regularly yet.

Downstairs in the café all the chairs and tables had been pushed to one side.

Madame Mons was wiping the floor, a cloth tied around her head. "You'll get your breakfast in a minute," she announced abruptly without looking up.

They had agreed the evening before that he would pay fifteen francs for the room and breakfast. He was to say in advance if he wanted any other meals, and that would cost another eight francs at the time.

He helped Madame Mons to put the chairs back in their places before asking: "Is your husband up already?"

"He's in the village getting bread."

He got no more than this one sentence.

She worked with jerky movements, gathering the dust together almost maliciously in a cloud before sweeping it up into a dustpan. "There he is," she said suddenly with a slight nod outside.

Robert sighed with relief and went to the door.

Monsieur Mons brought the Deux-cheveaux to a noisy standstill and squeezed out.

"Ah, *mon garçon,* today promises to be quite something. What heat! Compared with Nizier below, it's cool here. There it's like an oven, an oven...." Big drops of sweat stood out on his face, and his shirt was soaked through.

"Great heavens," he breathed out with difficulty and whispered to Robert at the same time: "the flower shop is in Mont Bleu."

"Alban...!" cried a shrill voice from inside.

"Yes, yes, I'm coming!"

"Where is Mont Bleu?" Robert asked.

"About two kilometers beyond Nizier."

"Alban!" The voice came for a second time.

"You will do it, won't you, eh?" He looked at Robert anxiously, as if he was afraid that the boy might have changed his mind in the night.

"I promised. But where is the cemetery?"

Robert took the loaves out of the car.

"Nizier," Monsieur Mons breathed hoarsely and patted him on the shoulder.

"Merci, *mon garçon,*" he called then. "Ah, you've got muscles. Just like I used to have. Should have seen me at the fair at 'Try Your Strength.' I beat everyone. They were frightened of me, *mon garçon.* They only had to look at me to be afraid . . . ."

"Oh, yes?" The voice sounded mocking. Madame Mons stood in the doorway, a contemptuous smile on her lips. "Of whom?"

"*Salope,*" muttered Monsieur Mons. "Bitch."

After breakfast Robert wandered down to the village. He had plenty of time to go to Mont Bleu and buy the rose.

The view was glorious. The wide valley stretched out before him, and he could see the glistening of the Isère down at the bottom. The mountains were hazy in the heat.

Nizier. That was the name of the village. It had taken him a week to find the place.

He had not told anyone the reason for his coming here, not even his parents. He'd been thinking about it for nearly a year, and a month ago he had at last made it a reality.

"I'm going on vacation to France," he'd informed his

surprised parents, "to wander around a bit on my own."

"Don't you want to come with us? You can bring a friend like last year."

"No. This time I want to be on my own."

"You're old enough," his father had said. "I did the same when I was your age. Make sure you have enough money, and if you ever get into trouble, just send a telegram."

Fantastic, his parents. They never went on at him and usually let him make his own decisions even though he was an only child. Just the same, he knew that his mother would have loved him to go with them to Scotland, but they had left the choice open to him.

She was there when he had found the notebook. Robert had been helping her to clear up his grandfather's apartment after his death.

His grandfather had been a doctor. Robert had been surprised at how tidy he had been. In the cupboard and drawers they had found notes about patients, everything in alphabetical order. There was a box by the letter M.

Robert opened the box and saw a small book and a bullet. Rather surprised, he'd picked up the bullet. It was small and weighed almost nothing. After that, he had leafed through the notebook and the first thing he read when he opened it was: *"I'm alive, I'm alive. God, how can this be true?"*

There was little else. A few sentences, some initials, a short comment, a name—Robert Macy. It was dated 1944.

He had gone through his grandfather's notes but there was no mention of the name Macy. He put the box in his bag and, that evening, when he and his mother had gone to eat in the Latin Quarter, had inquired:

"Does the name Robert Macy mean anything to you?"

"Robert Macy?" She had frowned and thought about it. "No, nothing. Why?"

"I came across the name today when we were clearing up at Grandfather's. He isn't a relation? After all, I'm called Robert, too."

"You were named after my brother. It must be one of the hundreds of your grandfather's patients, I suppose."

The waiter had arrived at that moment, his mother had ordered, and Robert Macy was forgotten.

In the months that followed, however, the notebook stayed in Robert's mind. It had an almost magical power of attraction over him.

Robert stopped for a while and looked around him at the mountains.

On one of the pages of the notebook, Robert Macy had scribbled:

Outside again this evening for the first time. The moon lit up the valley and seemed to bewitch Belledonne. Met Monsieur M. And a little farther on: *Monsieur M. hates me.*

Belledonne was the name of a mountain. He had worked that out. Who was the Monsieur M. who had hated Robert Macy? And why? There was no explanation in the notebook. What intrigued him most, though, was the end.

Tonight Pension Belledonne. Room Sixteen. Eleonore.

Robert started to walk on.

He had brought maps of the French Alpine region that

showed even the smallest hamlets. After that he had under-lined the places beginning with N, because somewhere in the notes he had found: *the village N.*

Then he had set off on his quest, searching for and ask-ing questions in villages that looked out on Belledonne. An old man in one of the villages close by had told Robert about the café that had been called the Belledonne, and after a week, he had ended up here.

The road was narrow and windy and got busier as he made his way down to Nizier.

He could see the village square below him now, and the church. Robert thought the churchyard probably lay behind.

On one side of the square was the *mairie,* the council house, with the post office next to it; on the other side was a shop, old and untidy-looking, with *supermarché* writ-ten over it in large letters. To the right of that was a café called *Chez Lucette.* A vine grew over the terrace. It looked cool. Robert decided he would have a drink there after he made his purchase. A bit farther up was an open spot to play *boules.* There were some men playing even at this early hour. Excited cries followed the dry clicks of the metal balls.

He had had no chance to ask Monsieur Mons how he should get to Mont Bleu, so he stopped a woman who had been shopping at the supermarket.

"Go right down the hill and then turn left at the main road."

He followed the woman's directions and crossed the

square. A long wall ran alongside him to the left. Behind that would be an estate, probably with a château or a large old mansion. He reached the main road quickly. Cars and trucks swished past. After a quarter of an hour he reached Mont Bleu and found the flower shop easily.

A small woman tottered determinedly around the brightly colored flowers, watering them.

"Voilà, Monsieur, we drink a lot in this hot weather, and they need water, too," she told him cheerfully. "You have to pamper them like small children. Talk to them a bit every now and again. It sounds strange, but it's true. A plant needs love and attention just as a person does. How do you give it to them? By talking to them. Now, what can I do for you, monsieur?" She looked at him expectantly.

Robert immediately felt embarrassed that he'd only come to buy a single rose, just one rose in this shop full of flowers.

The woman noticed his hesitation.

"Monsieur hasn't decided yet." She nodded helpfully.

"Oh, yes, I need a rose, a yellow one," he said quickly.

"One?"

"Yes."

"My, that's strange," she said thoughtfully, as she carefully took a yellow rose out of a bucket, "that's strange. Especially today ... that's what I call a coincidence. A coincidence, monsieur."

"A coincidence?"

"Yes, I can think of no other word for it. I know only one person who always bought a yellow rose. One rose, every time she was in the neighborhood. Occasionally, she'd buy a plant too, or a bunch of something, chrysanthemums or carnations. Never a bunch of yellow roses though. Never. She always wanted one of those. Heaven help me if it isn't true. *Mon dieu,* what am I saying, and today of all days?"

The woman quickly crossed herself. "The poor woman's just died, you know. She's being buried this morning. In Nizier; that's a bit farther up from here. That's why I find it a coincidence, Monsieur, that you should be buying a yellow rose today, you see? I'll wrap it up for you."

"Can you put it in a plastic bag?" he asked.

"Ah, now I see," the woman laughed understandingly. "It's to be a surprise, is it? You shouldn't be able to tell straightaway that it's a rose."

She was already tottering away, and she returned a moment later with a plastic bag.

"I was young once, too," she said. First she packed up the rose in cellophane and then carefully let it slide into the bag.

"Voilà, monsieur, I hope she'll be happy with it."

Robert paid and thanked her for her trouble.

The church bells were already ringing when Robert returned to Nizier. The mass for Madame Girauld must be about to begin. He was surprised at the number of people; this was a different village from the sleepy-looking hamlet of an hour ago. Soberly dressed people filled the square, gathered into various groups; others hurried straight into the church. The coffin must already have been taken inside. Robert had just seen a long black car slowly drive away.

He decided to go and have a drink on the terrace at Chez Lucette. He could wait there till the mass was over.

A couple of men were sitting at a table.

"It must be pretty busy there," said the tallest, nodding towards the church.

"Monsieur *le curé* has always dreamed of a pen full of sheep. Well, he's got what he wants today. He's in his element." The man who spoke these words was leaning back, his thumbs hooked behind his suspenders. He had a flushed face in which two bright eyes darted.

"Look, there's Madame de Béfort, too," another man commented. "She hasn't changed a bit. I've never known her any different from this."

"Except for that stick, of course."

Madame de Béfort . . . a tremor ran through Robert.

Madame de B. is completely to be trusted, Robert had deciphered at the opening of Robert Macy's notebook. The handwriting was not clear, particularly at the beginning. With difficulty he had read, *I can rely on her.* A *P.* came up and an *L.* Then *Eleonore,* the only name that was written out in full. The name kept coming up, sometimes in succession.

Robert followed the gaze of the man at the table and saw a small woman dressed in gray. She was walking slowly, leaning on a stick that she moved forward carefully.

"Apparently she's in agony sometimes," the bright-eyed

man remarked, "but she never shows it. She'd rather bite off her tongue than complain."

"How old would she be, Grolot?"

"Coming on for ninety, I think. But she's all there still, that I can tell you."

"A blow for Monsieur Girauld, anyway. I hear he's aged ten years. It was so sudden, too," the tall man commented.

"Yes, his daughter was everything to him, everything. He always adored her."

Monsieur Grolot turned and shouted over his shoulder: "Hey, Lucette, bring me another. Same as before."

A girl came out—a woman, in fact. She had a lively, expressive face. All her movements were easy and graceful. She was carrying a glass of white wine on a tray.

"Your stomach will get much too swollen with all this early-morning wine, Grolot," she teased.

Monsieur Grolot grinned broadly and folded his hands over his paunch, showing the curve.

"That's what I call the curve of bliss, my young girl."

Lucette laughed and turned towards Robert. A pair of light-brown eyes looked directly at him.

"Anything to drink?"

"A Coke, please," he said, a bit confused. He put the plastic bag down on the ground.

His eyes followed her. Monsieur Grolot noticed. He grinned again and raised his glass to him.

"Yes, my boy. I agree with you. A fine girl, that Lucette. She's the best we have here in the village."

Robert smiled shyly. Lucette came back shortly and put the Coke down in front of him.

"On vacation?" Her voice was warm and interested.

"Yes."

"Are you staying long?"

"I don't really know yet."

Singing started up from the church. The group in the café was quiet for a moment and listened.

"You can hear Monsieur *le curé* clearly again," Monsieur Grolot remarked, "he likes the sound of his own voice best. Of course, he'll do his very best for all that fancy lot from Paris. Just like at Easter . . . ." He grinned. "There was no end to it then. After mass he asked Madame de Béfort: 'Well, Madame, what did you think of it?' Do you know what she answered? 'I came to hear the voice of God, *mon père*. But you didn't give Him a chance. I could only hear yours . . . .' "

They laughed. "But how do you know that, Grolot? Were you next to her?" Lucette teased him.

"I heard it from her man, Pierre. You know very well that I only go at Christmas. Otherwise it becomes routine."

"Do you think her ex-husband is there too?" the tall man asked, and nodded towards the church.

"Madame Girauld's, you mean?"

"Yes."

"I haven't seen him. Strange, in fact, that everyone in the village goes on saying 'Madame Girauld.' Even when she was married to that man from Paris. That other name has never been used. Madame Girauld it was and has always stayed."

"I'll get another round," the tall man said. "We can still drink in peace now, but it'll soon fill up here."

Half an hour later, Robert stood up. He paid for his Coke and sauntered in the direction of the graveyard. His surprise was growing. How could a fellow like Monsieur Mons have had such a girlfriend? People had even come from Paris to attend the funeral.

Without his realizing it, he had reached the churchyard. It was bigger than he had expected. The white marble of some of the graves reflected the glaring sun. It made his eyes ache. Some graves were well tended, decorated with ostentatious artificial flowers that surrounded a photograph of the deceased. An occasional grave was even fenced off with iron, as if there were a fear of the dead escaping.

His glance fell on a black marble tombstone. It took up a large area and looked well kept. Shiny black marble. The family grave of the Giraulds . . . massive and impressive.

Would Madame Girauld's coffin soon be placed here? There was no indication to that effect. Perhaps this family just happened to have the same name. He could not imagine that Monsieur Mons's girlfriend belonged to this black marble.

The day grew even hotter. The sun burned down mercilessly and there wasn't even a breath of wind to relieve it. The path Robert was walking on was dry and dusty. He decided to look around, although he didn't have much time.

The church bells began to sound once more. Now he had to behave as if he were a visitor who just happened to be visiting the graveyard that morning. Which grave should he go and stand by?

He could hear footsteps in the square, shuffling, and some coughing. He walked quickly to a bench that he saw, and sat down. His hand unconsciously clutched more tightly at the white plastic bag.

First the priest appeared, his head held proudly, as if he wanted to show that death struck no fear into him. He was wearing thick-lensed glasses that made his eyes seem bigger, like big glass marbles. After him came the coffin, carried by men in black. Over the coffin lay a simple black cloth. Robert could see at a glance that there weren't any flowers or wreaths.

An old man walked behind the coffin. He had a stick, too, and his leg was dragging a bit. Next to him a younger man. His son? Then a young girl of about sixteen, he guessed. She walked hunched over, looking at the ground, a fixed, impenetrable expression on her face. She wasn't dressed for the funeral either, like the rest. She stood out among the dark clothes; a skirt and a checked blouse, her bare feet in sandals.

It was a long procession. Shuffling, and yet more shuffling, the shoes becoming dusty in the dry earth. Was the priest going to stop at the Girauld grave? No, he walked on. Only the old man turned his face sideways for a moment.

The mourners drew close to the bench where Robert was sitting. He got to his feet rather clumsily and the white bag slid off the bench and fell to the ground. He held on tightly to the back of the bench with one hand and bowed his head.

The coffin moved past, at eye level. He could only see the black cloth with its fringe. The girl trod on the plastic bag. It was too late now to pick it up. He tried to push it back with his foot.

Something curious was happening. The procession was obviously disturbed. People were looking at one another in surprise, there were whispers here and there.

"Where are we going?" he heard. "Do you understand it at all?"

The priest turned right to an unkept, overgrown part of the graveyard. The consternation in the procession increased.

Robert couldn't join them yet; that would seem too much of a coincidence. He must wait alone till the procession had all gone past.

It didn't take long. He heard the deep carrying voice of the priest and soon afterwards the people came back past him. Amazement was written all over their faces. They seemed to be hurrying to get away.

The girl was one of the last. Her expression hadn't changed. If anything, she was perhaps a little paler. She looked so out of place, it was as if she'd only chanced to join the procession. As she walked past him he noticed that her bare sandalled feet had turned gray in the dust.

29

*   *   *

Left alone, he stood up. He had to carry out his promise now. He walked quickly to the coffin. It was still above the ground, stripped of its cover. Around it was freshly piled earth. The hole had already been dug; the gravediggers would probably be here any moment.

All at once Robert felt affected. Here before him lay a woman whom he didn't know, not even her Christian name. A woman to whom he had to bring a final salutation in someone else's name.

Carefully, he took the rose out of the bag and removed the cellophane.

"This rose is from Alban Mons. He thanks you ... he thanks you for all your visits. He will never forget you," he said softly. Then he bent over and laid the yellow rose on the coffin.

He stayed there for a time, then straightened his shoulders. He was about to turn around when his eye fell on a gray stone which had begun to lean over slightly. Fresh earth from Madame Girauld's grave lay spread over the weeds and wild grass.

He stooped and deciphered the letters with difficulty.

Here lies Robert Macy, he read.

+++

chapter three

Robert just managed to find a place in the crowded café on the square. The talk was lively and excited.

"Mon dieu! I don't understand any of it!" cried Monsieur Grolot. "There's a man who has a family grave where you could lose a dozen and now he goes and buries his own daughter in a windy north corner. Doesn't make sense to me."

"It's not like Monsieur Girauld. I know him too well for that. His family is everything to him. When his son was killed in the war, he spared no cost to have him put in the family grave."

"It must have been another one of *her* ideas. I always

found her peculiar." The woman who said this pursed her lips disapprovingly.

"Peculiar, maybe, but she was a lady," remarked a man who had a gray moustache that he constantly played with.

"A lady, come now!" the woman retorted scornfully, "she always had men sniffing around. Didn't you see how many weirdos were at the funeral?"

"Ah, so that's why you couldn't keep your eyes still," Lucette remarked casually as she stacked glasses on a tray.

"You weren't even there," the woman answered. "And you know very well that I wouldn't do any such thing." She primly pulled her dress down over her knees.

"It wouldn't have done you any harm if you had," called out Monsieur Grolot, "even though you're successful enough without even having to ogle. I saw the fat Mons looking hungrily at you the other day."

The woman stared straight in front, clearly affronted.

"That Mons doesn't seem to stand a chance with that wife of his," said someone next to Robert, grinning. "Anyway, he wouldn't spare a glance for such a bag of bones as Dreu there. He prefers something like this, like Mireille. . . ."

The exaggerated gesture he made stressed the fact that Mireille was certainly no handful of bones.

"As for the daugther who came!" Mademoiselle Dreu began again, "I think it's a scandal. A scandal. She was dressed like a tramp, and at her own mother's funeral too."

"She hardly ever saw her mother. I heard that she's been living with her father since the divorce."

"Old Girauld never managed to get over that divorce," someone commented. "It's always bothered him."

"Her ex-husband, Trabut, was in fact at the funeral. Did you see him? He looked very upset."

"Then he was the only one," Mademoiselle Dreu snapped again. "Because that daughter didn't even spill half a tear. A hard case, if you ask me."

"Nobody did," Lucette flared up. "I know the daughter. Cristine's a nice girl. You can't judge someone by whether they cry or not. I know people who can produce waterfalls without meaning a thing." She glared at Mademoiselle Dreu.

Monsieur Grolot stuck his thumb up approvingly and grinned at Lucette.

"The death of his daughter must be the finishing blow for Monsieur Girauld," he remarked. "It's the first time I've seen him walking with a stick. And the funeral makes no sense at all to me. Why all alone at the other end of the graveyard?" he looked questioningly around the terrace.

"I don't understand it at all; not at all," he exclaimed again. "Those Giraulds are bursting with money, but I've never in my life seen such a lousy bare grave. No flowers, no wreaths, a cheap wood coffin. And not even in the family grave . . . . Same again, Lucette!"

Robert got up and paid. The heat, which was growing steadily more overpowering, and the excited voices around him were making him dizzy.

"Hey, you've forgotten something!" someone called after him. "Your bag!"

33

He picked up the plastic bag and walked slowly across the square. The sun beat down on him, he coud feel its rays fall along his back. Madame Girauld. Who was this woman? She was lying a meter away from Robert Macy.

So his "uncle" was dead. It had been a shock when he had read the name on that bit of weathered stone. *Here lies Robert Macy, born 1922, died 1944.* He had been twenty-two years old. Again the sentence from the notebook rushed into his head. *"I'm alive. I'm alive. God, how can this be true?"* Words from someone who had already been dead for years.

Robert stopped for a moment. The road before him wound upwards. He had not told Madame Mons that he would be eating. Should he go back to the village?

He hesitated in the middle of the road, a bit dazed by the heat.

He heard the sound of a moped approaching in the distance. He couldn't see it yet, but from the high screaming sound it was making, the rider was obviously going too fast. Dangerous with all these bends and the rather steep hill.

He moved to the side to wait for the moped to pass. Part of the tarmac here had recently been relaid and it was still covered with fine gravel. The sputtering came steadily closer. A figure appeared in the bend, crouched over the handlebars. The yellow crash-helmet flashed in the sunlight.

"Watch out!" Robert shouted. He could almost predict what was going to happen. The moped was going much too fast. It took the bend badly, went into a skid, turned on its side and flung its rider out onto the side of the road.

Lucky he was wearing a crash-helmet. The words shot through Robert's mind as he ran towards the rider.

He saw torn jeans and sandals before he recognized the girl from the funeral. . . .

Her arm had an ugly graze and she was bleeding. She loosened the helmet and threw it off. He tried to help her up.

"Go away, *allez-vous-en,* go away!" she shouted wildly at him. She tried to stand, but collapsed. "Go away!" she shrieked again, her face working.

She tried to get up again, but she couldn't. Then she let herself sprawl back and began to cry.

It wasn't the sobbing of someone suffering pain, but a deep, helpless noise that came from way inside. It was as if her whole body was weeping. It sounded frightening under the baking sun on the deserted road.

Robert knelt next to her and put his hand on her shoulder. "Don't move," he said gently. "I think there's something the matter with your ankle. It's swelling." He undid her sandal carefully. She did not even hear him, but sobbed and sobbed.

He looked around. The moped was still in the road. He quickly walked over to it and dragged it to the side.

The crying stopped as suddenly as it had begun. She was catching her breath now like a small child, and when she wiped her hand over her face, it left black marks behind.

He bent over again. "Let me help you."

"Go away," she said again, but this time the hard tone had gone and she sounded almost pathetic. Robert acted as if he hadn't heard her. Without a word he pulled her up.

"Try not to put any weight on your foot," he advised.

"I can't." She shook her head. "It hurts too much."

He let her down again carefully. "First I'll see if your moped's still working."

After a few tries he managed to start the motor. "At least this hasn't given up. I'll put you on behind and take you to the doctor."

She wiped her face again. "He won't be at home yet."

"How do you know?"

"He's at our place."

"Then I'll take you there."

"No."

He looked at her and waited.

"I don't want to go home," she said, just audibly. Her head was bowed. One leg of her jeans was rolled up. The bare ankle was still swelling alarmingly.

"You can't go walking around like that," Robert said. "Come to think of it, you can't even stand properly. Come on then, I'll take you to the pension where I'm staying." He pulled her up again. "Here, lean on me."

She followed his instructions meekly. When he'd lifted her onto the luggage carrier, she asked, "Why were you at the funeral?"

"I just happened to be there. I had to visit someone else's grave."

"Oh."

She was quiet for a moment. "You've forgotten your bag. It's over there."

"It doesn't matter. There's nothing in it."

He drove the moped very slowly up the hill.

"All right?" he kept checking, looking back at her. She nodded, and he could feel her clinging tightly to his T-shirt at every bend.

"What's your name?" he asked as they got close to the pension.

"Cristine. Cristine Trabut."

A watchdog couldn't have looked more dangerous, Robert thought when he saw Madame Mons waiting at the doorway. He braked carefully to a halt right in front of the stone steps.

"There's been an accident," he started to explain immediately before Madame Mons could even open her mouth.

"How many killed?" she spoke sarcastically.

Robert nervously turned to look at Cristine. What a time for her to talk about death.

"I've told you that I won't put up with girls," Madame Mons declared. "You're leaving now."

"But, Madame," he insisted. "She was thrown off her moped. Her ankle . . . see for yourself."

Madame Mons's eyes moved to Cristine's leg. There was no better proof. Her expression changed at once.

"That doesn't look good," she said gruffly. "Can you still walk?"

Cristine shook her head.

"Come with me." The old woman lifted the girl from the luggage carrier and carried her expertly.

Robert propped the scooter against the wall and followed the pair inside.

Madame Mons turned around at the kitchen door. "I don't need onlookers," she snapped at him. "I can manage alone."

The door was closed in his face. Robert looked in amazement at Monsieur Mons, who had been following the whole scene without saying a word.

"That's what she's like, *mon garçon*," he commented resignedly. "Unpredictable. At least you aren't saddled with her. I am. Who's the girl anyway?"

It was only now that Robert realized how strange it was that neither Monsieur Mons nor his wife had recognized Cristine.

"Cristine Trabut."

"Cristine Trabut?" Monsieur Mons gaped at him, perplexed.

"You mean to say . . . you mean . . . Madame Girauld's daughter?"

Robert nodded.

"But, *bon dieu,* what's she doing here? Shouldn't she be at home with the Giraulds?"

"After the funeral she went off for a bit of a ride on her moped," Robert explained. "She fell off on a bend not very far from here. I was close by. Luckily, she's got off quite well."

Monsieur Mons pulled out his handkerchief and wiped his forehead and neck. He looked at the closed kitchen door.

"*Eh bien* . . . in any case, she doesn't look like her mother. Not at all. I've never seen the girl, though I've heard that she always tears through the village on that thing when she's on vacation. No wonder she's had an accident. How was the funeral though? Did you do what I asked?"

"Yes."

Robert was suddenly overwhelmed by a heavy weariness. He felt no desire to tell Monsieur Mons at that moment what he had seen, how everything had gone. So much had happened that morning. The whole funeral had taken a hold on him in an inexplicable way. Then Robert Macy. He had hardly had time to absorb the fact that he was dead, too. That was because of the girl Cristine . . . that desperate outburst at the side of the road. There was something . . . he tried to find the word. Something lost about her. Yes, that was it. She gave the impression of being deeply lost.

Monsieur Mons must have sensed his mood because he didn't press the issue. He only asked, "Have you had anything to eat?"

"No, not yet."

"*La vieille* is still in the kitchen. We won't bother her just yet. When she's finished I'll get you something."

Almost a half hour passed before the old woman made a reappearance.

"There," Madame Mons said in a motherly tone. "Come

and sit here." She took a second chair and put Cristine's leg on it. "You'll see, you'll be walking again normally in a few days."

She smoothed her apron and patted her hair. "I'll make you some food. You must be hungry."

Robert watched in rising amazement as Madame Mons settled Cristine in a chair and fussed around her. Her whole behavior had changed.

"Your wife is very kind," Cristine remarked when Madame Mons had returned again to the kitchen.

"Yes, er . . . yes, of course," Monsieur Mons stammered.

Cristine looked better. Her face had been washed and her arm treated with iodine. An impressive-looking bandage was tied around her ankle.

"It's easy to see that your wife used to be a nurse," Cristine went on. "She's very competent."

"Yes . . . yes." Monsieur Mons didn't sound wholehearted.

"Really strange that I've never met her. But then, I'm not in Nizier so often. And this café is rather out of the way. Or is it a pension?"

"It used to be," Monsieur Mons replied. "We haven't rented any rooms the last few years."

"I've seen you somewhere before," Cristine spoke rapidly as if she were frightened of a silence. "At Mireille's. She made my communion dress and you were there when I went to try it on."

"I don't remember that," Monsieur Mons muttered, glancing anxiously at the kitchen door.

"It's a while ago, of course, because Mireille's been living in Voiron for at least five years. She's married to a baker now."

"Yes, yes. I heard something like that," Monsieur Mons whispered.

His face had turned deep red and drops of sweat were standing out on his forehead.

"I'm not surprised she married a baker," Madame Mons commented flatly. She came out of the kitchen carrying a tray with some bowls. "That Mireille always knew how to bake sweet rolls and there were idiots who let themselves be caught by that."

She nodded at the bowls. "It's not very special. Just leftovers." Her voice changed when she talked to Cristine.

Robert wondered whether she knew that Cristine was Madame Girauld's daughter. Probably not, otherwise it was unlikely she would have treated her like this.

"Robert hasn't eaten yet, either," Monsieur Mons threw out. Madame Mons glared at Robert.

"You didn't warn me. Well, go on then. It'll cost eight francs."

"I'll pay you, too," Cristine said quickly.

But Madame Mons would have none of that.

"Be quiet." She filled Cristine's bowl in a motherly but decisive way. "Eat up. It'll do you good."

It was a strange meal. Robert could not understand either Madame Mons nor Cristine. Neither of them mentioned the funeral.

They talked about everyday things. Madame Mons took

at least a quarter of an hour to explain how to make jam. *Confiture . . . .*

Cristine listened attentively, or at least seemed to.

"Eat up," Madame Mons said every now and again, and Cristine followed the order like an obedient child.

Meanwhile he had plenty of time to take her in. The others were not paying him any attention. He did not know whether he would call her beautiful or plain. Both, he thought. Because of the way her face changed expression. One moment, as she listened tensely, her face was fixed into a mask, then she looked questioning again and uncertain and her mouth would tighten as if she were on the point of bursting into tears.

She was slender, though he might of course be mistaken because of the loose blouse she was wearing. Her hands were small and bony and she crumbled her bread constantly. She bit her nails too, badly. When she noticed he was looking at them she clenched her hands quickly as if she felt trapped.

He went on wondering the whole time about what chord Cristine had touched in Madame Mons. Monsieur Mons was conspicuous by his silence and his noisy breathing, a regular heavy sniff.

"Can I stay a bit longer?" Cristine asked Madame Mons after the meal.

"Yes, all right. Come with me through to the kitchen."

She lifted Cristine from the chair and assisted her out of the room.

* * *

"If I live to be a hundred, I shall never be able to understand it," Mons said, glancing at the door from behind which came the sound of muffled voices. "She is and always will be a mystery to me."

The afternoon was slowly drawing to a close. The heat was stifling, just as on the previous day. Robert felt clammy and uncomfortable and longed for a cold shower.

He helped Monsieur Mons serve some tourists who wanted something cool. The fat man was visibly suffering in the heat. His face was swollen and red and sweat was streaming down his neck. Robert tried to look at him as little as possible, lest his longing for a shower grow worse.

"A mystery, *mon garçon,* an unsolved mystery," Monsieur Mons said and collapsed heavily into a chair. He greedily gulped down a glass of cold beer and wiped the foam from his lips.

"She's always like this if there's something the matter with someone," he explained. "You have to break a bone first or cut your head to coax friendliness or sympathy from her. That's how I got caught, years ago. . . ." He puffed heavily from across the table. "I had appendicitis. I would never have guessed that such a small thing could bring such misery. I was operated on, and who did I happen to have as nurse? Exactly. . . ." He motioned with his thumb towards the kitchen door.

"Nothing was too much trouble for her. Everything done in the same tone that you heard today at the table. To cut a long story short: I fell for her because I imagined she was always like that."

"How I cursed that appendix once I was stuck with her! What you can't understand is the way she changes completely when you're ill. As if she's fed up with healthy people. In the beginning, I used to try to fake. But she had that quickly taped. You can only be really ill or have something wrong with you, like that girl with her ankle. But believe me, as soon as that child is walking normally again and no longer depends on her, then it's over. Don't ask me to explain it. I can't. It's been a mystery to me for thirty years, and I'm unlucky enough to be married to that mystery."

Monsieur Mons fanned himself with the handkerchief. "That she should have had an accident with the scooter," he went on, "and today too. The day of her mother's funeral. I wouldn't have recognized her, but as I've already told you, she doesn't come here so often."

"What was her mother really like? Did you know her well?" Robert inquired cautiously.

"Know her well?" The childlike eyes in the red face lit up. "I knew her to be a woman that you rarely meet, *mon garçon.*" He sounded sad.

"What do you mean?"

"You'd have understood at once if you'd met her. She was very special and there was something . . . something secret about her. Every word that came from her mouth took on a different meaning, even the simplest phrases. She lived in Paris, but sometimes came to stay with her father, Monsieur Girauld. She always used to come here when she was in the village. I would see her coming . . . ."

44

Monsieur Mons's voice broke.

"Ah, *mon garçon,* I know what you're thinking. That fat Mons had an eye on her. No, that wasn't the case. It was more than that. I would never have dared lay a finger on her. For that she was too . . . too . . . ."

He groped for the word but couldn't find it. "When she came," he went on, "she would only look at me, and say . . . 'It's good to be here,' a simple sentence that means nothing in particular, you could say. I would have found it ordinary too if it came from anyone else, but not from her because there was something special about her.

"She only needed to say those words and I'd feel myself getting lighter. I'd quickly bring her a chair. If the weather was fine she'd sit outside where she could see Belledonne. If it was cold she'd find a place inside by the window so that she could see the snow caps. Then she'd order tea. Always tea . . . I used to sneak out to Grenoble and buy the best teas for her. I'd also make a mixture of different sorts; she loved that. She never said so, but I felt it all the same, because she said nothing. She would hardly ever speak. That silence, though . . . ah, that silence told me a lot.

"I never judged her the way they did in the village. She was divorced, you see, and traveled a lot. She was an archaeologist. In Greece and Egypt and those sorts of places that you see on television. They gossiped a lot about that in the village, but I never joined in. They thought excavating was man's work and not for women. They were just jealous, *mon garçon,* because you only had to look at her to see that she was a real woman. I know for sure that she sensed that

I never judged her. That's why she'd come here. I'm sure of that. She had a yellow rose with her sometimes. She'd put it down on the table when she drank her tea . . . ."

The childlike eyes stared into the distance.

"I asked her once: 'Why do you always have a yellow rose and not a red one?' It was difficult to ask the question because, you know, she'd be far away with her thoughts and I didn't want to force myself on her. You needed courage to ask her anything.

" 'I don't like red,' she said. 'Red is the color of blood.'

"Who says that kind of thing? Only she could. It sounded as if she had told me in confidence: 'Alban, you're the only one who knows this, and that's why I don't like red.' That forms a bond, you see. I've never talked about this to anyone. You're the only one now who knows it. You've only just come here and you don't even know her. In any case, she isn't alive any more . . . ."

Robert had listened closely to the unbroken stream of words coming from Monsieur Mons. So Madame Girauld had never been his girlfriend! Only a visitor who wanted to enjoy the view.

"Once something happened, *mon garçon,* that I shall never forget. *La vieille* was at her sister's in Lemiers, thirty kilometers from here. This was last autumn and it was terribly misty.

"Madame Girauld appeared suddenly out of the mist. It was as if she were stepping out of a big gray-white cloud. With a yellow rose. There wasn't a mortal soul to be seen.

46

"She went to sit at the window as usual. I brought her her tea and then she suddenly asked: 'Would you mind if I had a look at the view from one of the rooms?'

"I remarked that she wouldn't be able to see anything in the mist. 'I'll look through the mist,' she said.

"I can remember it word for word. I took the keys and we went upstairs. She stopped outside room sixteen, and I gathered that she wanted to go inside. I couldn't see a thing when I threw open the window and shutters for her. There was a mist hanging that you could almost touch, gray all over.

"She stayed in front of the open window and wouldn't even sit. 'Would you mind leaving me alone for a little while?' she asked then.

"I implored her not to stay long or else she'd catch cold. Just the same, it was an hour before she came down again. She looked completely numb with cold.

" 'Drink a glass of wine with me, Monsieur,' she said. 'Only if it's on me,' I answered. That was bold of me and I was afraid for a moment that she'd refuse, but she only smiled and so I understood that she agreed.

"I went to the cellar and took out the best bottle that I had. A *Châteauneuf du Pape* '49, a very good year. I couldn't care less if it cost me a week of raging rows with *la vieille*.

"I opened the bottle and filled the glasses. 'Madame will come back when the mist lifts,' I said. 'You can't see a thing.' She didn't react but told me that she'd be leaving again the next day.

"When she'd gone I went upstairs. Twice up the stairs and my grave is almost dug, but, fine, I did it for her. For myself, too, because *la vieille* would ask otherwise what the window was doing open.

"Room sixteen was empty, of course. Not a chair or cupboard out of place. Only the rose. She'd forgotten it. It was on the bed. I took it downstairs and put it in the bottle which we'd drunk from together. Sentimental, you might say. Perhaps, but, you know, when you're old and fat then there isn't much left to get sentimental over. Particularly if you have a wife like mine. *Enfin,* I had to throw away the rose when *la vieille* came home the next day, otherwise there would have been misery to have from it."

Monsieur Mons gestured helplessly.

"Do you know that she isn't in the family grave?" Robert asked.

"Not in the family grave? Not with the Giraulds?" Monsieur Mons stared at him, aghast.

Robert shook his head.

"Where then?"

"In a corner of the churchyard." Robert hesitated. Should he tell Monsieur Mons what he had seen? That she was lying next to Robert Macy's grave?

Before he could make up his mind the kitchen door opened.

"Alban, this girl needs to go home. You must take her."

"Of course, of course." Monsieur Mons was already heaving himself up from his chair.

"I'll come with you," Robert offered quickly.

Madame Mons carefully helped Cristine to the car. Her sandal didn't fit any more because of the thick bandage, so she carried it in her hand.

++

chapter four

The Giraulds' house lay a bit outside Nizier. It was large and looked rather somber. Gray stone, covered here and there with ivy. A wide drive with plane trees on either side leading up to the front of the house, where some cars were parked. The Deux-cheveaux's brakes squealed as Monsieur Mons brought the car to a standstill before the door.

The door was opened immediately. An elderly woman, dressed all in black, hurried out toward them. When she saw Cristine she burst out, "Where have you been? Where have you been? Everyone's been worried about you, your grandfather most of all. The man's upset enough as it is. Why did you have to do this to him?"

Cristine shrugged her shoulders indifferently and did not answer.

"She's had an accident," Robert explained.

"An accident! Now that as well!" the woman complained. "As if the day wasn't sad enough as it is."

At that moment two men appeared. One was close to fifty, the other was old and leaning on a stick.

"What happened, Cristine?" the younger man asked.

"Nothing happened, Papa. I fell off the moped. This boy happened to be close by and he took me to Monsieur Mons's. His wife took care of me. Everything's all right. Don't worry."

"You ride far too recklessly," the woman interrupted, "the whole village disapproves."

"Enough, Berthe," the old man said. It sounded like a command.

"It's good to have you back again," he continued, talking to Cristine as she passed him, supported by Robert and her father.

"Please come in, too," he invited Monsieur Mons with a gesture as he followed them inside. Monsieur Mons waddled in after the old man and awkwardly mumbled his condolences.

"We're all sad about it," Monsieur Girauld said. "It happened so unexpectedly, too." He sounded exhausted.

There were still a few people in the large room that

they now entered. Relations or friends, Robert supposed.

Cristine was seated in a chair. Apparently unmoved, she stared ahead of her, only reluctantly answering the questions that were fired at her.

"Let her be," the old man ordered. "She's back. That's the most important thing."

Cristine threw him a grateful look.

Robert looked around. They were in a room full of old French furniture; a sofa with deep red velvet upholstery. Stiff-looking chairs had been grouped around some slender-legged tables. There was also a display cabinet with some bowls and fragments in it. He wanted very much to have a closer look.

Family portraits hung on the walls, most of them in gilded oval frames. One of them stood out. It was a modern painting of a woman. The colors were exuberant and warm. A woman in a garden under a striped parasol. She was dressed in blue. The sun twinkled on the trees and splashed out onto the grass. The canvas had a sparkle about it, but at the same time the eyes of the woman seemed to hold a message. It was as if those eyes did not see the sunlight, as if they were looking far away.

In one hand she was holding a yellow rose . . . . .

Robert was so preoccupied with the painting that he did not even hear Monsieur Girauld's question.

"I'm sorry," he stammered, when he became aware that the old man was talking to him. "I was looking at the portrait."

"That's my daughter. She was buried this morning."

"Yes, yes, I know," Robert murmured awkwardly. He wanted to add something, but couldn't find the words.

"I asked if you'd like something to drink," Monsieur Girauld repeated.

"Please." Robert went on standing there woodenly and heard the same question being asked of Monsieur Mons.

The fat man looked as if he felt ill at ease in such surroundings. He was sweating more heavily than ever. He was speaking twice as loudly as usual to cover up his shyness. He was having a conversation with Cristine's father.

"Yes, your wife, Madame Girauld, often used to come to us," he trumpeted. "She loved walking, didn't she? I always used to say to her: 'It does you good, a walk like that.'

" 'Yes,' she would answer, 'I love walking, I could walk for hours. I love the view of Belledonne.'

"She always used to come to look at the mountain. Alas, that's all in the past now. Yes, indeed, all in the past. I knew your wife, Madame Girauld, very well, though."

Monsieur Mons pulled out his handkerchief and energetically wiped his face and neck with it.

"Doesn't that fellow know they were divorced?" Robert heard someone next to him whisper. He suddenly felt pity for the sweaty man who looked so grotesque amidst these walls filled with staring portraits. In his confusion the fact that Cristine's father was divorced from his wife must have slipped his memory. Luckily, Monsieur Girauld intervened.

"Would I like a drink?" Monsieur Mons brayed. "Please, Monsieur, yes, please. Kind of you to offer something under these circumstances. It's a sad day, isn't it? For the

53

whole family. What am I saying? For the whole village, Monsieur. Your daughter was much loved, ah *oui,* much loved."

Monsieur Mons was just getting into his stride, but Monsieur Girauld interrupted him firmly, wanting to know what exactly he should pour for him.

"Something with a lot of water, a lot of water, please. *Mon dieu,* how hot it is. Hot enough to die from. Oh, I'm sorry, I didn't mean that." Monsieur Mons rather miserably gesticulated in apology.

"I still have to thank you," Monsieur Girauld changed the subject, "for looking after my granddaughter."

"Oh, that was nothing," Monsieur Mons waved the thanks away, "a small matter."

The woman in black came in with a trayful of glasses. She looked contemptuously at Monsieur Mons, but he did not notice.

"I'm also grateful to you," Monsieur Girauld turned to look at Robert. "Are you here on vacation?"

"Monsieur Robert has rented a room with us," volunteered Monsieur Mons before Robert could answer.

"Hasn't that pension of yours been closed now for a time, though? Are you renting rooms again?"

"Only to Monsieur Robert." Monsieur Mons laid his hand in a comradely way on Robert's arm. "We've made an exception for Robert. An uncle of his had in fact been to our pension before. A long time ago. He claims it was at the end of the war. Have I got it right, Robert? What was your uncle's name again?"

"Robert Macy."

"Ah, *oui,* Robert Macy. His uncle . . . ."

Monsieur Mons stopped abruptly and stared with wide open eyes in Monsieur Girauld's direction. The old man suddenly seemed to have lost his balance. His arms were reaching out uncertainly as if they were seeking support in the room. The stick clattered on to the parquet floor.

"Mon dieu," cried the woman in black. "Monsieur, Monsieur . . . !"

She rushed to him and, together with Robert, led him to a chair.

"It'll pass, it's a dizzy spell," Monsieur Girauld slurred and closed his eyes. He was breathing with difficulty.

Cristine sat paralyzed in her chair, deathly pale. Then all of a sudden she got up, limped to her grandfather's chair and fell down before him. Almost in despair she clasped him to her.

"Bonpapa, not you! Not you!"

"A doctor!" called a woman. "Get a doctor! Get Doctor Perrin! Quick!"

Late that night Robert got up and put on the light. A mosquito was pestering him. His watch said half past two. He stayed sitting at the edge of the bed, sleepy and miserable. He should never have drunk so much. How rotten he felt. His head roared and the room moved strangely. The mosquito struck against the sheets not a meter away from him. He wanted to grab a towel and pulverize the rotten creature to a spot of blood. He got up warily, but his movements were too slow and the mosquito zoomed away with a whine.

Slowly he let himself sink back on the bed and closed his eyes. Events ran around each other, words swayed through his thumping head. Half sentences, then a scream again.

A scream. "Bonpapa, not you, not you!"

That was what Cristine had cried that afternoon, yesterday afternoon. She had rushed from her chair and hobbled to her grandfather.

"Not you!"

He had observed the scene speechlessly. The old man, dazed in his chair, breathing with difficulty, and Cristine before him, still crying out. The woman in black had pushed her roughly to the side. He later found out that she was the housekeeper.

"Stop that screaming, girl," she snapped at Cristine, "you're only making it worse."

"The doctor," she ordered, "get Doctor Perrin. It's certain to be his heart."

"I'll go," Monsieur Mons had stammered with dismay. In his rush, he pushed against a chair, which crashed to the floor.

Monsieur Girauld was carefully lifted and taken to another room. Robert and Cristine were left behind alone. She seemed extremely upset and audibly bit her nails. He had seldom felt so ill at ease. The muffled voices in the passage, the quick footsteps and Cristine across from him, biting her nails.

"Stop that," he had said without thinking.

"I . . . I can't help it." She clenched her hands into fists again. "I can't do anything about it. Do you think he's going to die?"

She spoke quickly, looking anxiously at him.

"No, of course not. It's the heat and the tension of the funeral."

"Do you think so?" Her face relaxed a little. "Do you really think so? He's never had anything like this. My grandfather's hardly ever ill."

"Everyone's bothered by the heat, even Monsieur Mons. You've seen that yourself."

He went on calming her with soothing words for as long as he could think of anything to say. Then silence fell, a silence in which Cristine began again to bite her nails, and he searched desperately for something to say that might comfort her.

Monsieur Mons came back with the doctor who went straight through to the other room.

Just before Robert left, Cristine said: "Hey, you will come again, won't you?" She suddenly seemed rather helpless again and looked uncertain.

He nodded.

"Tomorrow?"

"Good."

He'd turned around for a moment at the door. God, how upset she looked there in the chair in the middle of the room. Then he and Monsieur Mons left together.

Robert chased the diving mosquito once more. It

wouldn't escape this time. His hand moved heavily when he lifted it. The mosquito circled away. Dratted insect. The effort made his stomach turn. Why had he filled himself up with wine? Because he'd been so depressed?

First he'd gone for a long walk outside Nizier, but the damp heat had only made him thirsty and had not thrown off his somber mood. He had walked to the square. The terrace was filled with people, all talking cheerfully. He had looked for a place in the corner and Lucette had come. Lucette with her open smile and direct gaze. Her hips swung as she walked, and she had long brown legs. He wasn't the only one to look at them.

He had ordered a carafe of wine and it was empty before he knew it. As the evening wore on, he had drunk another one empty, too.

Monsieur Mons was sitting at the kitchen table when Robert got to the pension. "Watch out for *la vieille*," he had whispered to him as he stumbled inside.

"I'll make you some coffee," he said at once, taking in the situation at a glance.

Robert had sunk into a chair and hazily followed Monsieur Mons's movements as he threw water into the coffee pot. His actions were so different from Lucette's supple swaying that Robert had suddenly broken out laughing, a stupid sobbing laughter.

"You're really on your last legs," Monsieur Mons had said, and at the word "legs" Robert had choked, swallowed, coughed, and wiped away the tears from his cheeks.

"Eh bien, *mon garçon,* the wine's coming out of your ears. You're really blotto. Here, drink your coffee."

A big bowl had been pushed towards him. He gulped down the burning hot black drink.

Monsieur Mons looked at him, shaking his head.

"You should thank the Lord that *la vieille* isn't here to see you in such a state. She'd throw you out tonight."

Robert gestured carelessly and knocked over the bowl.

"Do you think . . . do you think that Madame de B. means Madame de Béfort?"

His tongue had felt as if it filled his mouth, the words came out with such difficulty.

"You might well be right, there," Monsieur Mons said and grinned.

"And Monsieur M.? Are you Monsieur M.?"

Monsieur Mons's face twisted into a widely beaming moon.

"You're a bright one. I'm Monsieur M. From Monsieur Mons, get it?"

"Yes, yes," Robert blubbered. "And Eleonore? Who is Eleonore?" The full moon bent forwards till Robert could nearly pluck the grin off it.

"That's *la vieille, mon garçon. La vieille.*"

Monsieur Mons rocked with laughter.

"La vieille," mumbled Robert, flabbergasted. "That old woman."

"Do you think you can get upstairs on your own?"

Monsieur Mons asked. "I can't go up the stairs again. I've already had enough effort for today." He hoisted himself up and took Robert's arm to support him.

"Monsieur Mons, thank you," Robert slurred.

"You've had a fair amount tonight," Monsieur Mons grinned. "Your parents should have seen you . . . ."

He pushed Robert in the direction of the stairs and waited just long enough to hear him stumble into his room. Then he shuffled back to the kitchen.

Robert turned on his side. He felt as sick as a dog. Hot and cold at the same time.

What a vacation! This time last year he'd been sailing on the Frisian lakes with a couple of friends.

Lakes, water. No, don't think about water or boats. Boats move, heave on the waves. Waves, high waves. You're swept up high and then sink back to the depths.

He felt it coming. He got up, swallowing. The room spun around, the bed sloped sideways. He reached for the stoneware bowl.

+++++++++++++++++++++++++++++++++++++++

chapter five

The next morning Robert drank countless cups of black coffee to take away his hangover, and considered how he should start his investigation, and whether there was really any point to it.

Robert Macy was dead and had been for a long time. But how had he died, and did he have a family? Now that he had started off by saying that Robert Macy was his uncle, he had to stick to it, Robert had decided.

Monsieur Mons had also told the Giraulds that. It would be impossible now to come up with another story. It would sound too farfetched.

Later that morning, sitting opposite Madame de Béfort, Robert suddenly found it very difficult to pose the question he had come to ask.

He had been disappointed to learn that she already had a visitor. However, she had greeted him with a smile after her housekeeper had ushered Robert into the sitting room, although she made no attempt to introduce him to the other older woman who was already there.

"You've got a visitor," Robert observed. "I'm afraid that I've come at a bad time."

"I have indeed got a visitor. Madame Leclair and I are neighbors," said Madame de Béfort. She motioned him to take a chair and invited him: "Sit down and tell me who you are."

Robert took a seat. He felt very uncertain. A heavy weight pressed down on his stomach.

"I'm Robert Reuling," he began, hesitantly. "I'm from Holland, The Hague, and. . . ." his voice caught.

"I understand you want to ask me something," Madame de Béfort helped him.

"Yes, Madame. . . ."

"*Oui?*" The yes-word told him she was waiting. He had to say something.

"Did you know a person called Robert Macy?"

The reactions of the two women were different. Madame Leclair, who was wearing a hat, stared through him in obvious displeasure. Madame de Béfort, hunched up in her chair, became more attentive and her eyes lit up, a fact that did not escape Robert.

"Robert Macy?" She spoke carefully. "How did you come by that name?"

"He was an uncle of mine."

The blood rose to Robert's cheeks as he said the words. He felt that it would be difficult to deceive the woman across from him.

She remained silent for a moment. She looked searchingly at him, her eyes cool and detached.

"Really?"

This one word gave him another chance. But he could no longer go back.

He swallowed. "Yes, Madame."

"Your 'uncle' died a long time ago." She stressed the word "uncle" very emphatically.

"But how and where did he die?"

"Surely you know that? You are his nephew, aren't you?"

It sounded sarcastic. She stood up suddenly and said brusquely, "I shall let you out."

Robert stood up too; he was completely confused and did not know what he should do. The command was not one to be misunderstood. He quickly took his leave of the woman in the hat, who nodded stiffly to him.

Madame de Béfort walked before him. Her stick tapped on the wooden floor.

"Don't bother, I'll do it myself," she said to her housekeeper who hurried toward them.

"Madame, I . . ." Robert stammered, but he did not go on.

The words stuck in his throat.

She did not even turn around, but tapped on toward the door.

He made a last desperate effort: "Madame . . . ."

She held the door wide open for him and did not even say good-bye.

He went out, head bowed, and heard the door close behind him.

Dr. Perrin's car passed him as Robert trudged slowly towards the gate where Cristine's moped stood. He still had to take it back.

The first visit of all that he'd paid to someone from the notebook had been a total failure. Madame de B. He was sure that it was she. He remembered Robert Macy's words, *"Madame de B. is completely to be trusted . . . ."* She had known him but would not give anything away because she had realized that Robert had not been telling the truth.

Had he been alone with her he would have told her the truth. Of all the times for her to have had a visitor!

He hesitated at the gate. Go back? No, certainly not now. Perhaps another time. If she'd see him, that is. He started the moped and rode to the square.

It was quiet on the terrace at Lucette's. There were only a few men sitting at a table. They had been there yesterday, too.

Robert leaned the scooter against a tree. Grins appeared on all the men's faces as soon as they caught sight of him.

"Voilà, here comes our Romeo!" called out Monsieur Grolot.

"The poet!" cried another. They laughed uproariously and beckoned him over.

"Will you have something to drink? Then there'll be something else worth hearing."

Robert did not really understand. He walked towards the table. They shook his hand jovially.

"Alors, well then, did you sleep well?" The question was accompanied by a smack on the shoulder.

"Not badly," Robert muttered. "I believe I drank a bit too much last night," he admitted.

"You still look pretty pale. Comes from hanging around Lucette's skirts."

"Lucette?" Rather taken aback, he looked from one to the other.

At that moment Lucette appeared. She looked less vibrant in the hot pale daylight than she had the evening before. She had put up her hair which made her look a bit older. There was a good-natured expression on her face.

"Allez, haven't you anything better to do than pester the boy?"

She looked at Robert rather curiously. "Would you like anything?" she asked.

Robert nodded.

"Don't give him any more wine, Lucette, or else he'll take you again for Eleonore. . . ."

Monsieur Grolot smacked his thighs. "My, she must

have been quite something." He put his arms on the table and gazed yearningly at Lucette: "Eleonore .... The way you walk .... Your hips, Eleonore ...."

He wanted to go on, but Lucette gave him a push.

"Enough."

Robert felt his back prickle with sweat.

"Did I call you that?" he stammered.

"As if that was all!" Monsieur Grolot exclaimed again, and everyone laughed so loudly that he realized dismally that he had definitely not stopped at that one name.

"Lay off," said Lucette again. She laughed slightly and walked back inside the café.

"I'll come too," Robert muttered, and hurried after her.

"Keep an eye on him, Lucette," Monsieur Grolot called out behind them. "He may look like an innocent calf but he has the intentions of a bull."

"What on earth did I say last night?" he asked when they were alone.

"Ach, they're only teasing you. They don't really mean any harm," Lucette evaded the question. "What would you like? A Coke?"

He nodded and ran a hand through his hair. In heaven's name, what had he jabbered about last night?

Lucette wiped the top of the bottle and poured the fizzy liquid into a glass.

"I didn't insult you, did I?"

"*Alors, ça.*" She looked at him almost tenderly. "What's your name?"

"Robert."

66

"Insult, you said? *Mais non,* Robert." She shook her head and leaned on her elbow on the counter. "Who is Eleonore? Your girlfriend?"

"No."

"Someone you're in love with?"

"No again."

"The name probably just came into your head?"

"Probably."

"Do you think it might suit me? Eleonore . . . ." She looked at him, half laughing, half waiting.

He hesitated.

"Shall I answer for you? You're thinking in fact: No, that name doesn't suit her. But you're too well brought up to say that, especially when you're sober." She laughed outright now and ruffled his hair a moment.

"Eleonore . . ." She repeated the name thoughtfully. "The name doesn't suit someone who runs a café like me. Can you imagine them calling out, 'Hey, Eleonore, two beers,' or, 'Give me another glass of wine, Eleonore . . . .' No, it doesn't fit."

"I find Lucette just as beautiful," said Robert. "More beautiful even."

"You say the nicest things even without alcohol," she laughed.

Robert began to feel more at ease again.

"I see you're riding Cristine's moped. Do you know her?"

"I met her yesterday for the first time."

"At the funeral?"

"No, afterwards. She had an accident on her scooter. She skidded and I happened to be there just then."

"It wasn't serious, though?" Lucette looked worried.

"She came out of it all right. Just a few fair-sized grazes and a swollen ankle. I took her to Monsieur Mons's pension and then we brought her home."

Lucette shook her head and started to wash glasses.

"Cristine's a sweet girl but you have to get to know her better. They aren't too keen on her in the village. Nobody likes her racing around on that thing nor the way she looks. Those old hags only notice her clothes and the old men don't think she's got enough meat on her bones, and they don't look any further. Nobody takes any trouble over her or gives her a good cuddle from time to time. She needs that badly because, if you ask me, she's never had it. She's always had to manage on her own, just like me in fact, but I can cope better with it. What do *you* think about her?"

"Who? Cristine?"

Lucette nodded.

Robert sipped his Coke thoughtfully.

"I can't really say. We've hardly spoken to each other."

"Do you intend to see her again?"

"Probably."

"*Eh bien,* Robert, listen then." She leaned forward over the counter and took his wrist. "You're here on vacation, eh? A tourist. And you want someone to have fun with, *s'amuser un peu,* as we say. I'm asking you one thing: don't go upsetting Cristine if you don't mean anything by it because she's worth more than a vacation." She looked almost unfriendly and the grip on his wrist tightened.

"Why did you say that?"

"Why? Because I've been on vacation, too. Not so very long ago either. A fellow whispers a few soft words in your ear and you've had it. 'Specially if things aren't too good at home, like with Cristine. That makes you only too gullible if anyone's sweet to you. She'd walk in with both feet. Cristine is no Eleonore any more than I am. The only difference is that I'm old enough not to fly into it and Cristine isn't yet."

She let go of his wrist abruptly and hurriedly started to dry the glasses.

"I told you I found Lucette more beautiful than Eleonore, didn't I?"

"Leave off that kind of talk." She gave a brisk wave.

"You're very keen on Cristine, eh?"

"Yes."

"Why?"

She looked at him, a slightly brooding expression on her face, and slowly shrugged her shoulders.

"Does everything have to have a reason? I don't know. Just because."

"Hey, Lucette, is anything else coming?" a voice called from outside. "You're leaving us without anything to drink. You mustn't warm up the poor lad like that, he's already got it badly enough."

Lucette winked at Robert.

"Don't mind anything those fellows say."

She took a bottle from the shelf, filled a carafe with water and went outside. A moment later Robert heard the terrace rock with laughter.

He wanted to pay for his Coke when Lucette came back inside.

"Leave it," she said. "It's on me."

"Thanks. That's nice of you." He stayed there hesitantly, looking at her. "Tell me, Lucette. I can hardly remember a thing about last night. What did I say to you?"

Lucette grinned. "That's really bothering you, isn't it? Well, as you want to know so badly, here goes. You didn't just call me Eleonore, but you said that my legs weren't too bad and that I swayed my hips in a way that you could not close your eyes to."

"Did I . . . did I really say that?"

"You're blushing, *mon petit.* You're getting even redder than all that wine you swallowed yesterday."

"Did I say that when everyone else was there?"

"Don't worry so. You really weren't noisy. You were rather a nice drunk. It's just that some people around have sharp ears for some remarks."

"I don't remember a thing," mumbled Robert. "I only remember walking along a road at one point."

Lucette laughed and her eyes were teasing. "I put you on it myself.

" 'What should I do?' you asked me. I said 'Walk.' 'That's easy,' you remarked.

"Just the same, I made a sign of the cross, hoping that you'd reach the fat Mons's."

"I'm sorry, Lucette. You weren't angry, were you?"

"Me? I'm used to all sorts. And, you know, no woman feels insulted if you like her legs or her hips. Or else she's as hypocritical as the plague.

"Allez, I have to work now, you've already held me up long enough." She turned away.

"Hey, Lucette?"

"Now what?"

"I think you're beautiful even when I've only had a Coke. And you walk in a way that must stir up all Nizier."

"Eh bien! And at four o'clock in the afternoon, too! It must be the heat."

"On top of all that, you're nice."

"That's the last straw." She laughed good-humoredly.

"Now get the devil out of here or else I'll let you pay for your Coke. See you, Robert. Say hello to Cristine."

Robert changed gear and accelerated the moped. He had tied the helmet on behind. A mild wind blew through his hair as he headed toward the Giraulds' château.

How good he felt all of a sudden. He'd seldom felt so good, free and light. Was it because of Lucette? He had never dared say anything like that to anyone else—Marjo, for instance.

He used to think it a victory back home if he sat next to Marjo, with her slow, drowsy gestures when she tossed back her hair or lit a cigarette. He did not even want to talk to her, only to touch her, and he didn't even dare do that.

Marjo . . . she flirted with every boy and treated him just like the rest. He could be thoroughly sick of her sometimes, and yet at the same time, find her irresistible.

Everything about Lucette was natural. Easy and spontaneous and warm. Was that because she was so much older? She must be going on thirty. But she was not self-conscious, which made it easier to make you feel at ease. Nothing sounded silly when you talked to her.

Marjo . . . . Come to think of it, this was the first time he had given her a thought since he had come to Nizier.

Robert let go of the handlebars and flourished his arms in the air. He gripped them again quickly as the scooter lurched. If he didn't watch out the same thing would happen to him as to Cristine. He saw it all already; he and Cristine opposite each other, both with bandages around their ankles. Madame Mons in nurse's uniform, a tender, caring expression on her severe face. Or, at least, for as long as the bandages stayed on. Robert choked with laughter but the reckless feeling left him as he went up the drive to the Giraulds'.

✛✛

chapter six

The elderly housekeeper opened the door.

"I've come to bring back Cristine's scooter. How is she?"

"A little better." The statement came out reluctantly.

"And her grandfather?"

"The doctor will be here at any moment."

It was clear that she had no intention of letting Robert in.

"May I talk to Cristine?"

Before she could open her mouth, he heard a voice call from inside: "Is that you, Robert?" A moment later Cristine hobbled into the passage.

"Back to your chair," the housekeeper commanded, "the doctor says . . . ."

"He says a lot," Cristine observed indifferently. "Come on in, Robert."

The housekeeper shrugged her shoulders and left with an injured expression on her face. Robert followed Cristine, who limped to a chair.

"How are you?"

They were in the same room as the day before. The room seemed even bigger because there were no other people. His eyes unconsciously slipped back to the painting of the woman under the parasol.

"Much better," he heard Cristine answer.

"And your grandfather? I couldn't get much out of your housekeeper. She is the housekeeper, isn't she?"

She nodded.

"She isn't very friendly, is she?"

Cristine laughed. All at once she looked nice. "You shouldn't take too much notice of her. I don't. My grandfather's much better, luckily. He got up already this morning. He's resting now for a little while and the doctor's coming later, though he thought that was nonsense. He's never ill."

"Can you walk at all yet?"

"Just a little."

"Do you fancy a ride?"

She stared at him in amazement. "Are you saying, I mean, er . . . ."

"We'll do a duet. Together, on the moped. I don't want

to spend the afternoon with those ancestors of yours. They can hear everything we say. Here," He got up and offered his arm to her, "hold tightly onto me and we'll try to slip away without anyone seeing us, because I'm sure that housekeeper would try to prevent it otherwise."

He helped her out of the chair. "I've got you. You open the front door, quietly," he whispered to her.

"Doesn't your foot hurt?" he inquired anxiously when they got outside.

"Not at all. I can't feel a thing."

"Quick, put on your helmet."

"What about you?"

"I like it more without, and I won't be going fast."

Robert kept turning around as he drove.

"All right?"

Cristine couldn't hear, but she could guess what the question was, and she nodded. The road was narrow and windy. Robert eventually turned off down a sandy path and stopped. Cristine took off her helmet.

"Hey, it's good here. Much better than being inside."

"If you wait there, I'll come and get you." He leaned the moped against a tree, walked back to her and lifted her up again.

"You certainly don't weigh much," he said. He carefully let her sink down onto the grass. From this shady spot they could look down over the still hazy valley.

"Look, there's the church," Cristine pointed.

He followed her finger. "And there to the left is Madame

de Béfort's estate. You can just see a bit of the wall. A bit higher you've got the Leclairs' house. That new gray roof."

He nodded.

"How long are you staying in Nizier?" he asked.

"Till mid-September. Then school starts again."

"You live in Paris, don't you?" He fell back in the grass and folded his hands under his head.

"Yes, with my father."

"My mother's from Paris. My grandmother lived in Le Marais. Rue de la Bretonnerie. Do you know it?" he asked.

"It's quite near l'Ile de la Cité, I think."

"That's right."

"We live close to the Bois de Boulogne."

Robert was silent. Should he mention her mother? Weird, in fact, that Cristine didn't even know that he had put a yellow rose on her mother's coffin. He couldn't possibly tell her that.

"Did your mother die here? In Nizier, I mean?" he asked cautiously.

She nodded and he noticed her face change at once.

"Were you there?"

"No."

She wound a blade of grass around her finger. He could see the gnawed-off fingernails..

"Was it her heart?"

Cristine shrugged. "Maybe."

"Why maybe?"

She wound the blade of grass more tightly around her finger and the top of it turned deep red.

"I don't think she felt like it any more."

"Felt like what?"

"Like going on living."

"What do you mean?"

"Just what I said. She didn't feel like it any more."

"Did she . . . ." Robert half sat up.

Cristine slowly unwound the blade of grass. It left a clear mark, and the top of her finger stayed red for a while.

"Commit suicide?" She looked straight at him. Her eyes seemed darker because of the shade of the tree. "No, not suicide. That wasn't her style. I always think that people who do that kind of thing must be living under great pressure. I could be wrong, of course. After all, I don't know much about it. But my mother was never tense or under pressure. She wasn't anything. Anything. She was . . . she was . . . ah, what does it matter?"

She shrugged again, apparently indifferent, but her mouth twitched nervously.

"Did you know your mother well?"

"Nobody knew her. Nobody."

The abrupt statement was bitter.

"But you can't just die like that, for nothing."

"All right, then. Her heart stopped. I know she took pills for her heart. It stopped suddenly while she was sitting in a chair. Just staring out into space, as she often used to sit. She never even suffered. At least, that's what everyone says. I didn't see her again." She turned her face away.

He saw the back of her head, and she started to bite her

nails. He wanted to talk about something else but did not know where to begin.

He put his arms around her shoulders carefully, but she pushed him away, almost angrily. When she turned back to him, he was shocked. Her eyes were burning strangely.

"I have to tell you something, Robert. Nobody else knows about it. Nobody. But I have got to tell someone, or else . . . ."

"What is it?" His uneasiness grew.

"I used to hate her sometimes . . . I really hated her sometimes . . . ." Her face twisted, turned ugly.

"You didn't know her. You've only seen that portrait; I saw you looking at it. Everyone admired her. She was beautiful, but she was only a shell."

"What do you mean?"

"There was nothing inside. No feelings, no . . ." Cristine began to stammer. "There was no warmth inside. She was empty. So empty that I sometimes wanted to hit her . . . ."

Robert felt an enormous tension in the last sentence, a tension that was all at once reflected in Cristine's whole appearance.

"My mother loved no one. And nothing. Not even my father or me. She didn't once protest when my father claimed me after the divorce. Not once. Don't you think that's strange? Nor later either. She thought it was all quite all right. It left her unmoved."

Cristine's voice took on a hunted, nervous tone. "She had a flat in Paris. I used to call on her sometimes when she was at home, but it was awful when I was there because we'd have nothing to say to each other. At least, she wouldn't. I really wanted to talk, but I couldn't because I always felt she was behind glass. I could see her but not reach her, I mean really touch her with my feelings. It's difficult to explain. And every time she saw me she used to look surprised, surprised that she had a daughter. Even I was surprised. I think I was just an accident. Too late to do anything about."

Robert wanted to interrupt, but Cristine was already hurrying on.

"There was one time I went to see her, a few months ago. A man was there, too. That was nothing unusual. Men were often hanging around, but never for very long. I don't think she had affairs with them, that's what's so strange. Sometimes I wished she would. She might have changed if she had really fallen in love with someone. Anyway, I came, and this man, I think he was called Pierre or Philippe, I don't exactly know any more, did his best. Towards me, too. He was nice and he really tried. I could see that, but my mother didn't even notice or didn't want to notice. You never knew with her.

"I got furious all of a sudden, really furious. I told that Pierre or Philippe that my mother was a block of ice, the only difference being that ice melts in the sun. He blew up and defended my mother. I began to shout at him, but really I was shouting at her.

"She just sat there . . . just sat there . . . ."

"Cristine!" Robert made a move towards her, but she did not see him. It was as if she was reliving that afternoon.

"I screamed at him that I hated her, hated, hated. It was awful.

"Then why do you come here?" he asked.

" 'Because perhaps one day she'll hate me too. Then at least she'll feel something,' I shouted, 'but there's nothing inside her, you'll find that out soon enough. You only see the beautiful mask. I'll show you there's nothing there.' "

Cristine rocked the top half of her body the way people do when they are in pain. "Do you know what I did? I went to a cabinet and took out a vase. I knew it was nearly three thousand years old. Someone had told me that. Not my mother, but someone else. I hurled the vase to the ground right in front of her. Then something else too, a bowl, I think. I can't remember any more. Pierre, or whatever he was called, pulled me away. He shook me hard. If only *she* had done that. But she didn't do anything! Why couldn't she get out of her chair, why couldn't she hit me or kick me out? She'd excavated that vase herself . . . ."

Cristine's voice broke.

"I called up the next day, as I didn't dare go myself. My mother said she'd rather I didn't go there again. I cried out over the telephone that I was sorry, that I would never do it again and all sorts of things like that, and that I would stick the vase together again, but she never once reacted." She wiped her eyes roughly.

"Didn't you see her again after that?" Robert asked.

"Yes, just once. About a month later. I always used to walk through her street to see if she was at home. I'd do that every day. I could tell from her car whether she was there; she had a light-blue Citroën. I saw it and I rang the bell. She opened the door and let me in . . . ."

Cristine's lips trembled.

"And then?" Robert prompted gently.

"She looked tired," Cristine faltered, but went on. "That made a pleasant change because my mother's face was always the same, smooth and calm as if she never went through a thing, never experienced anything. She told me she was going on a trip.

" 'Excavating again?' I asked.

" 'Yes, excavating again,' she answered.

"The way she spoke was different. It's difficult to explain. There was something about her tone. She was uncertain and she bumped twice into a table. She'd never do that kind of thing normally. I know nobody who moved the way she did; there was nothing sudden or brusque about her.

" 'I don't understand what you see in all that excavating,' I said. 'The past is over now.'

"Then something strange happened." Cristine faltered again.

"She stopped suddenly in the middle of the room and looked at me. She looked at me and she really seemed to see me for the first time—you must believe me. It all sounds so unlikely. She was seeing me for the first time, I could tell from the look in her eyes. I felt . . . I felt . . . as if I was being born . . . ."

She swallowed convulsively a few times and went on: "I wanted to say something to her, but the words wouldn't come. We just stood there looking at each other. Silly, really . . . .

" 'You've grown,' my mother said, surprised, and I just nodded and nodded. That was all I could do.

" 'Have you got a boyfriend yet?' she asked a bit later.

"I nodded again, but I was lying because I had absolutely no one.

"She asked me what his name was. 'Jacques,' I said, 'he's called Jacques.'

" 'Tell me something about him. What does he look like?'

" 'Dark hair,' I stammered, 'and he's a bit taller than I am. He's got brown eyes.' I invented a scar on his left arm and said that he played tennis, that he was very good at that and that we used to sneak off to the movies together. I even mentioned a Hitchcock film that I'd seen on my own.

" 'Does your father know about him?' she asked.

" 'No, nobody does,' I told her. 'Only you.'

"My mother went to sit on a sofa and I crept up against her. I felt so clearly that she was actually there. She even took my hand and looked at my nails. 'You mustn't bite your nails,' she warned me quietly, and I explained how I couldn't really help it. I just bite them without thinking, whenever I'm nervous or frightened.

" 'Are you frightened or nervous now?' she asked.

"I said, 'no,' but meant 'yes,' because I was nervous and extremely confused because I was talking to her for the very first time, but the conversation was a lie because Jacques didn't exist. I didn't dare to tell her how frightened I was that she'd go back into herself again. So I kept quiet. We sat there on the sofa for a while. I leaned very close to her and we talked: I can't remember any more exactly what we talked about. She was rather muddled, yet she seemed to me to be talking more clearly than ever before. She talked a bit about the past, but she jumbled everything up.

"I can remember her saying something about a horse called Josline and talking about my grandfather. She spoke about him with admiration. About his courage in the war and how he had saved so many people.

" 'Very many,' she said, 'not everyone, of course, that wouldn't be possible, but very many just the same.'

"I wanted to know more about her though, and I asked: 'What about you, Mummy, what did you do during the war?'

"I wish I had never asked that question. I could feel her change again. I didn't even have to look at her to feel it.

"I threw my arms around her and rocked her backwards and forwards. 'Don't leave me,' I begged, 'Please stay with me, stay with me.' But it didn't help. Her face disappeared behind glass again and she was a shell once more . . . ."

Cristine broke off. Robert looked at her narrow back and hunched shoulders and above that her mid-length hair, damp from the heat. She looked so helpless and alone.

Without hesitating, he pulled her to him.

"I may not understand it all," he said, "but I think you loved your mother very much."

She buried her head in his neck and sobbed and sobbed just as she had the day before.

"Cry," he said, "go on and cry. I'll stay with you. I won't leave you."

He rocked her back and forth like a little child and spoke comfortingly to her. Broken-off sentences, odd words. They were sounds meant to soothe her rather than anything else.

Eventually she grew quieter.

"I don't even know why I've told you all this," she said, wiping her face. "I hardly know you."

"Does that have anything to do with it?"

She looked at him and slowly shook her head. "Maybe not."

She was quiet. Everything around them was still. The leaves hung motionless on the branches. The oppressive heat seemed to stifle even the sounds.

Robert lay on his back and shut his eyes. Yellow and black spots appeared, yellow and black spots. He suddenly felt exhausted.

Cristine's mother was so different from his mother. He thought of how his parents had let him go off on his own. Fantastic!

Nizier. A dot on the map. Barely marked. In the two days he'd been here the village had already shaken him to his depths. Events and emotions had followed each other too quickly.

Nizier and Cristine.

He opened his eyes and turned his head sideways. She was lying next to him. Her face was so young and so close. They looked at each other in silence. At last he raised himself slightly, propping himself up on his elbow.

"When your ankle's better again I'll take you into the mountains," he promised. He stroked back some hair that had fallen over her cheek. She smiled tremulously.

"Watch out, there's an ant on your neck," he warned her. His fingers gently stroked her skin, but got caught in a thin chain she was wearing, a gossamer-fine chain with a round medallion.

He turned the gold medallion over and looked at it.

He caught his breath.

Eleonore, he read. *Eleonore.*

✤✤✤✤✤✤✤✤✤✤✤✤✤✤✤✤✤✤✤✤✤✤✤✤✤✤✤✤✤✤✤✤✤✤✤✤✤

chapter seven

There had been no hint of a storm when he had brought Cristine home. Now Robert ran; the sky had turned an ugly black, and a traitorous wind had blown up in the mountains. Rain beat fiercely against him in hard silver streams, and the whole time the storm thundered and lightning flashed.

What he was doing was dangerous. He would not be able to reach Nizier now. There wasn't a roof anywhere for him to shelter under. He went on running, his breath coming in short gasps. There was a short vivid bolt of lightning, followed by a crackling blow. What a storm it was! He'd never been in such raging weather before. One moment it was black everywhere, the next it changed to burning yellow.

The storm crashed, screamed and roared around him. Something cracked nearby. Sure to be a tree. He pushed on farther and ducked as low as he could into a ditch. Twigs beat against his face. He was soaking wet through and through, and frightened.

The storm seemed to die down for a moment but then the noise came back in all its intensity, worse than ever. He waited for it to pass, head between his arms. A roaring started up around him. Was the earth roaring too? He raised his head. Rocks? Falling boulders? Oh, God, no, not that!

The violence absorbed him. Suddenly he felt as if he were being pelted with stones. He hunched up, in pain, and tried to crawl farther away to find protection. It was hail. Huge hailstones!

The hail stopped just as suddenly, and everything around him went quiet. Robert stayed there. The silence increased but he had no strength left to get up.

How much longer did he remain there? One second, ten minutes, an hour? Time had ceased to exist.

At last he raised his head. The evening was fresh and clear, the skies cleansed.

He got up stiffly and looked around. What a mess! You could see that even in the twilight. The ground was covered with lumps of ice. He picked one up in his hand; it didn't even melt right away. Trees had been blown over and the path was strewn with branches.

He shivered. His clothes were soaking. There was mud all over his face and arms.

Robert set off towards Nizier.

The terrace at Lucette's was deserted. Bits of glass were lying scattered on the ground and a window was broken. The café door was open, but when he went inside there was nobody to be seen. There were no electric lights on, either, but he could see a candle gleaming in the kitchen.

"Lucette?" His voice sounded hollow in the dim empty room.

There was no answer, and he called her name again. Then he heard hurrying footsteps and a moment later Lucette appeared. Her hair was wet and tangled, her blouse torn, and her skirt dripped water.

They stared at each other for a moment in amazement.

"Mon dieu, what's happened to you?" Lucette cried out. "You weren't out in that storm, were you?"

Robert nodded.

"I'll give you some dry clothes in a minute, but you have to help me first. It's my uncle. He refuses to come out."

"Your uncle?"

"Yes. He's in the cellar, and that's flooded now. He's mad, you see."

Robert stared at her, not understanding.

"Mad? Who's mad?"

"My uncle. Oncle Lucien. Raving mad but quite harmless. Wouldn't hurt a fly. It's only that if there's a thunderstorm he creeps into the cellar because he gets frightened. I'm terrified he's going to drown because the cellar's half flooded. He's nearly up to his waist in water. Quick."

He followed Lucette in the semi-darkness.

"There has been a power failure. That happens quite often in bad weather," Lucette told him quickly as she went down some stone steps. "I've got a flashlight."

A confused shout met them. "He's very frightened now," she explained. "You have to be especially careful not to excite him."

"Bang, bang, dead!" shouted a voice in the darkness, "bang, bang, dead!" It came from a corner somewhere.

Lucette shone the torch around the half-flooded cellar. There were some planks drifting around and a few pans were bobbing up and down a few meters away from them like ducks in a pond. The wine racks had half disappeared under the dark water.

Lucette aimed the beam of light into the corner where a small man was wildly splashing the water. It was spattering all around his ears.

"Oncle Lucien, it's me, Lucette. You know, your niece. Come here, come here." She stretched out a hand to him.

Oncle Lucien looked weird. His round, bald head seemed even more naked in the glare of the flashlight. His mouth was hanging open and his eyes were two frightened round holes.

"Bang, bang, dead!" He splashed the water again.

"You'll kill yourself if you stay there," Lucette grumbled. "The thunderstorm stopped a long time ago, Oncle Lucien. You needn't be frightened any more. Come out now, or else you'll catch cold."

Lucette waded towards him, talking quietly all the while.

"I've brought a friend. He's called Robert and he comes from Holland. You know, where that cheese comes from that you like so much. You had some on Sunday. I'll give you a piece if you come out, I promise." Her voice was coaxing. "I'll even give you a whole kilo, but you have to come here first."

Oncle Lucien gaped at Robert. There was a moment's silence. He babbled quietly to himself. Then Robert waded after Lucette through the ice-cold water.

All at once Oncle Lucien began to beat the water wildly around him again. "Bang, bang, dead!" he screamed again. He stretched a hand out to a wine rack.

"*Merde,* not that," Lucette hissed. "He'll be flinging all the bottles into the room soon. That happened once before. We have to grab him before it gets that far. Help me."

She shone the flashlight right into Oncle Lucien's face, trying to blind him. Robert ducked past Lucette. The water splashed. Oncle Lucien, surprised by the sudden movement, screamed and fell backwards. Robert gripped him tightly.

"Monsieur Moustache, Monsieur Moustache!" Oncle Lucien shrieked desperately, trying to ward something off with his hands.

"Hold him tight," Lucette gasped. "Hold him good and tight. He'll calm down once he's upstairs."

90

She took one of her uncle's arms and drew it around her neck.

"*Allez,* Oncle Lucien, we're nearly there. Just a bit more paddling and we'll be on dry ground again."

They pulled the little man up the steps together. Oncle Lucien had turned limp and docile in their hands and was babbling nonsense. Lucette put him in a chair in the kitchen.

"You're a nice one," she said to him as she began to pull off his socks and shoes.

Oncle Lucien grinned innocently and looked down help-lessly at the floor where a big puddle was forming. Then Lucette pulled down his trousers.

"Don't just stand there, help me," she snapped at Robert. "I can't get these wet trousers off."

They undressed him in silence and Lucette dried him off and pulled him into his pajamas. Then she took him to bed.

When she came back she found Robert with Oncle Lucien's shirt still in his hands. She looked for another candle and lit it.

"Do you live here alone with your uncle?" he asked.

"Yes."

"How can you?"

"What do you mean?"

"Well, eh . . . he's mad."

"Quite. Mad as a hatter. But what do you think I should do then? Put him away? Because his five senses aren't ex-actly in line any more?"

"He was about to fly at you with that bottle down in the cellar. In fact, he's already done that." Robert nodded at her blouse.

"He was frightened," she snapped.

"But what would you have done if I hadn't happened to come along?"

"Ah yes, if, if . . ." Lucette shrugged carelessly. "If my aunt had had a moustache she would have been my uncle. You could go on like that. You came at the right moment. What more do you want?"

"Talking about moustaches—who is this Monsieur Moustache that he's so afraid of?"

"I haven't a clue. He must have known someone who was called that once, who frightened him. Whenever there's a heavy storm he starts shouting, 'Bang, bang, Monsieur Moustache.' You don't get much more out of him than that. When the skies start clouding over I say to myself: 'Here comes another visit from Monsieur Moustache . . .!'"

Lucette laughed, but then her face became serious. "You won't say anything in the village, eh, Robert? I mean, nobody needs to know anything about this. If they did they might want to put him away and I'd find that rotten for him because he's goodness itself. He's been like this ever since I was a child, and one way or another I've got attached to him. Perhaps there's a screw loose in me too somewhere, but I'd miss him if he weren't around."

"But aren't you frightened of him when he carries on like that?"

"No, not frightened," Lucette said. "Do you know what's strange? When he starts shouting the way he did this evening, I sometimes get the feeling that his sanity comes back for a few seconds. He's scared just like a normal person, dead scared. You saw that yourself. It's only once in a while, mind. When Oncle Lucien is, shall we say, 'normally mad' again, then he's always contented and he has a grin stretching from ear to ear."

Suddenly she burst out laughing. "We must look like a couple of idiots, too. Two drowned kittens. I'll get you some dry things. You'll have to wear Oncle Lucien's; there's nothing else. If you'd like a shower to wash off all that mud, go ahead. You'll have to take it in the dark, though, because we'll probably have hours to wait yet before the electricity comes on again."

Lucette opened a drawer, then hunted for something in a cupboard and pushed some clothes into his hands.

"I'll lead the way." She took the flashlight again. The stairs upstairs creaked. Heavy snoring came from one of the rooms. Oncle Lucien, guessed Robert.

"Here it is." Lucette opened a door. "You take the flashlight; I know the way like the back of my hand."

She smiled at him in the gloom. Shreds of emotions welled up in him, all jumbled up together. He wanted to say so much to her, but words always fell short. As soon as you said them they took on the color of lies.

"Does everything have to have an explanation?" she had said herself this afternoon. Did you have to put into words a warm feeling that suddenly swept through you for someone?

Lucette was quiet. Did she understand what was going on in him now? She lifted her arm and put her hand against his cheek.

"Even though I've only just met you, I like you too," she said. "I like you too . . . ."

When he came back downstairs, Lucette was in the kitchen. She had changed into jeans and a sweater. "The fire engine's busy going backwards and forwards. There must be a lot of hosing out to do. Lots of places flooded, I would say." She grinned when she saw him in Oncle Lucien's clothes.

"You don't look particularly sexy in those trousers. The crotch is almost around your knees."

Robert laughed.

"I bet you haven't eaten anything yet," she said. "Go and sit down and I'll give you something."

As she spoke she put French bread on the table and took out various cheeses from the cupboard. Then she sat down opposite him and propped herself up on her elbow on the table. Two candles flickered between them.

"Tell me about the storm. Why were you so foolish as to stay outside? You could have found shelter, couldn't you?"

Robert broke off a piece of bread and spread butter over it.

"I was just in a spot where there weren't any roofs to be seen. I'd gone for a bit of a walk."

"On your own?"

"Yes. After I left here this afternoon I went to Cristine's and I took her off on the moped. We talked for a long time, outside the village somewhere. Then I brought her back home and went for a walk. The storm took me by surprise. I've never seen anything like it and, to tell the truth, I was pretty scared."

"I can well imagine. You get really bad storms here in the mountains."

Robert broke off another piece of bread from the loaf, which was rapidly growing smaller. His stomach felt like a big hole. He tried not to gorge the food.

"Would you like something else?" Lucette asked when the bread was finished.

"Please. I'm so hungry," he confessed.

"It's all that emotion. First being caught right in the storm and then mad Oncle Lucien on top of it. You don't go through that every day. I'll fry you some eggs . . . ."

She got up and went to the cupboard. A moment later the kitchen was filled with the smell of fried eggs. He could hardly remember enjoying that smell as much as he did now, and at the same time he was gripped even more fiercely than before by the whole scene: the dimly lit kitchen, Lucette at the stove with her back to him, the candles on the table. Lucette, who had asked no more questions about Cristine . . . . She obviously thought that was now *his* business.

He experienced the moment with deep intensity and wanted to hold on to it, but realized he could not.

Lucette put a plate in front of him and pushed more bread towards him. Then she filled a glass with beer. She took the pan off the heat and scooped out the eggs.

"I like to see someone eat who's really hungry," she said and sat down opposite him again.

"Has your uncle been like that a long time?" he asked a bit later.

"I've never known him to be anything else but mad. He was normal before, though." She grinned for a moment. "Well, as normal as a person can be. Just the same, he isn't unhappy being mad, I'm sure of that. Happier than some normal people walking around this village."

"What did he do before?"

"He was the postman. He knew everyone and everyone knew him. My mother told me about it. He was familiar with every bit of ground, every path and shortcut in the area. Now the poor man can hardly find the way to his own bed."

"But how did he get like that?"

"The Germans got hold of him at the end of the war. Just outside the village. If you go up to that café of the Mons's, there's a ravine on the left. Not so very deep, but deep enough to break your neck.

"Well, they got hold of him there, the bastards. He still managed to save his neck, but that's just about all you can say. His brains had such a shake-up that he hasn't been able to tell *a* from *b* ever since, let alone decipher an address to make sure a letter gets to the right place. My mother took him in then because she wasn't married. She always used to say: 'It's better to live with a good madman than with a bad husband.'

"She had made a mistake about my father. He was worthless. He even collaborated with the Germans. He made off with all her savings and we never saw him again. My mother was left with the baby—that was me—mad Oncle Lucien, and debts, because that was all my father had left behind. She worked herself to death. I helped her as much as I could and we were eventually able to buy this café.

"She wanted to be independent, my mother . . . . Well, she was, but only for a while because when we'd been here a year she was taken ill and within a month she was lying on the other side of the square, next to the church."

Lucette nodded towards the window. "At least she's at peace there and has no more worries in her head, or so I believe. She had enough of those in her life, *la pauvre.*"

It was quiet for a moment.

"And you?"

"Me?"

"Are you happy?"

Lucette raised her eyebrows. "My, you are profound all of a sudden. Why shouldn't I be happy? Yes, I'm quite content . . . ." She smiled into the room. "About all sorts of small things. Like watching you sitting there gorging yourself, for example. That gives me pleasure and makes me feel good. Or when I see Oncle Lucien sitting in the sun, his bald head shining like polished furniture. When folks are gossiping on my terrace and shouting to each other. And also ...." Lucette laughed heartily, "also when I fall out with Monsieur *le curé* and he reads me chapter and verse. That's fun. I don't understand how the man can get so excited.

"He can't bear my short skirts," she confided to Robert. "He's always tripping over them, short as they are.

" 'You are jealous, completely jealous, Monsieur *le curé*,' as I always say to him, 'because you can't wear them yourself. I shouldn't like to go around in that sack of a black dress either.'

"Do you know what he says then?" Lucette leaned over the table, her eyes shining.

" 'Our Dear Lord does not approve of your dressing like that!'

"Well, I ask you .... He's surely got other things to do than measure my skirts with a ruler, and that's what I told him. 'Anyway, our Dear Lord wasn't as strict as all that as far as clothes were concerned. He sent Adam and Eve into the wilderness with only a leaf. I'm pure next to them!' "

Robert threw back his head and laughed out loud.

"I enjoy things like that." Lucette took a sip of beer from his glass. "Call it happiness, if you like. They're small things and perhaps not very important, but they make me feel good."

She looked at him, smiling.

"Why aren't you married?" he persisted.

There was a moment's silence.

"You want to know why? *Eh bien,* Robert, you'll get the answer for nothing. Because the man I fell for was married and had six children."

"And?"

"I only found out by chance because he didn't live in the neighborhood, you see. I told him that he had to make the seventh child with his own wife." She spoke ironically. She was quiet for a moment and then shrugged her shoulders. "I've spent sleepless nights over it. Cursed him, his wife, and his six children, too. But even that feeling passed and when I saw him much later I was glad I hadn't got myself stuck with him. He really had followed my advice because he'd meanwhile got himself eight children!"

She shook her head.

"And now? Isn't there anyone?"

"You're really curious. No, there's no one. I don't even find it so terrible to be alone. Perhaps you think that's strange, but it's really true."

Robert slowly finished his beer.

"What about you? You want to know everything about everyone else, but you don't give a thing away about yourself."

"There isn't so much to give away."

"Really?"

"No."

Lucette raised her eyebrows so high that her face ended up looking quite comical.

"Then why did you put a yellow rose on Cristine's mother's grave?"

"How do you know about that?" Robert's words shot out.

"So you did."

He did not answer.

"Why?"

"I can't tell you."

"There, you see? You're not giving anything away. Did you know her?"

He shook his head. "How do you know I did that, though?"

Lucette leaned on her elbow on the table and bent forward slightly.

"When you came here yesterday to have a drink, you were carrying a plastic bag in your hand. A stem was sticking out. I saw you go to the churchyard and when you came back the bag was empty. I ran after you because you'd left the bag on your chair, remember? Everyone was talking about the funeral, you heard that yourself. Why she wasn't in the family grave ... how there were no wreaths nor flowers ....

"I went to have a look myself in the afternoon. There wasn't anybody there then. I'd picked some flowers from the garden. After all, I had known her, even though only vaguely. Then I saw the rose and that made me think ... you came back to the café in the evening. You poured wine down yourself. It occurred to me that you might have developed a passion for Madame Girauld and you were now drowning your sorrows.

"To be honest, I did think you were rather on the young

side for her, but you hear so many strange things nowadays
. . . until you started up about Eleonore. That didn't make
sense because Madame Girauld's name was Pauline. Who's
Eleonore?"

"I don't know. Honestly, Lucette, I don't know."

"But how did you come across the name?"

"I read it somewhere."

Lucette looked thoughtfully at him and said nothing.

"I don't know whether I should believe you," she said at
last, "though it doesn't bother me one way or the other."

She stood up and started to clear the table.

Robert stood up too. "I have to go now. It's late. Thank
you for everything, Lucette."

She brushed away his thanks and walked to the door
with him.

"See you, Robert," she said.

++++++++++++++++++++++++++++++++++++++

chapter eight

Monsieur Mons was waiting up for him again. Robert could see him through the dimly lit window, sitting in a wooden chair, his sad, heavy body spilling over it, his arms stretched out in front of him on the plastic tablecloth. He was staring into the flickering candlelight.

The electricity must have been cut off here, too, Robert thought.

Robert tapped softly on the window pane. Monsieur Mons heard the noise and looked around. When he saw it was Robert he heaved himself up and opened the door.

"What have you been up to?" he grinned. "Last night

you could hardly stay on your legs and now you turn up in a set of clothes that could be your grandfather's."

"I was caught right in the middle of the storm," Robert explained. "I got thoroughly wet, and I was covered with mud. I had to pass through the square and then Lucette very kindly lent me some of her uncle's clothes."

"So you know her already, too?" Monsieur Mons remarked. "You're getting to be quite a villager. Would you like a drink?" He went to the refrigerator and took out two warm bottles of beer. He took the tops off quickly as if he were frightened that Robert might refuse.

"What a gale," he said and started filling the glasses. "We've been sitting here for hours in the dark, but I think we've still come off lightly. Or, at least, as far as I can see. There are a couple of shutters loose and two panes are smashed. But who knows, maybe there'll be more surprises tomorrow. I have to make do now with a candle stump that you can hardly read a newspaper by. *La vieille* has crept into her nest out of sheer misery and I can't say I blame her."

Monsieur Mons seemed to need to talk. "You've been at Lucette's then, have you? Did you see that uncle of hers? You can't get much madder than that, but he has a good life with Lucette. To be honest, I have to admit that I'd rather like to be in his shoes, simple though he is. At least I'd have something beautiful to look at then. God almighty, she's a juicy bit, that Lucette. Well, can you understand her not being married? They buzz around her like flies around syrup, but she keeps them all at arm's length. Always goes her own way.

"Well, have you found out anything yet about that uncle of yours?" he asked.

"Yes, I've found his grave."

"Have you now! Here in Nizier?"

Robert nodded. "He's at the end of the graveyard, next to Madame Girauld."

Monsieur Mons stared at him, open mouthed.

"Next to Madame Girauld? Well, I call that a coincidence! Next to Madame Girauld . . ." he repeated.

"He's been dead a long time. He died at the end of the war."

"Next to Madame Girauld . . ." Monsieur Mons said again. "So, without realizing it, I was the reason for your finding out where your uncle was."

Robert changed the subject. "How long has Dr. Perrin been living here in Nizier?"

"About six years. And that's six years too many, if you ask me. A completely different type from Dr. Pascal. Now there was a good man! That Perrin is always pompous and he mows you down with Latin words that mean absolutely nothing. Or else he always wants to stick needles into your skin or take your blood. The leech, I call him. No, give me Dr. Pascal any day. He was a man with a heart, all heart."

He pushed the candle farther away and piled the top half of his body onto the table. "All heart," he repeated. "Knew exactly how to treat his patients and no jabs or messing about with your body. Used to come in without any instruments. No, he did have a pipe. He carried that around with him day and night. It wouldn't surprise me if he hadn't operated on someone with that thing in his mouth. He often didn't even bring the gadget with the tubes, you know . . . ."

"A stethoscope," Robert suggested.

"That's it. He was unbelievably careless and he sometimes used to lose it, but you could forgive him that. 'No need for a stethoscope, Alban,' he'd say then, 'unbutton your shirt. I can do just as well without.' Then he'd tap your chest with his eyes shut because he said that made it easier to hear, and it was true, too.

" 'Clear as a bell,' he'd say after a while, 'clear as a bell. You're just too fat, man. You eat too much. I could prescribe a diet, but you wouldn't keep to it.'

"When I asked him then why I had heart palpitations, he'd pinch me and whisper: 'Probably been looking too much at Lucette. All the fellows who go near her have something wrong with them, either it's their hearts or it's high blood pressure . . . .'

"That pipe, eh," he went on. "You could tell from that pipe whether it was serious.

"There was a story that went around that he'd had a friend who'd been in an accident. He was in a mess and was in the hospital. Dr. Pascal sat by him day and night. His pipe stayed out. But suddenly, in the middle of the night, he lit up. Smoking was strictly forbidden there, but he never was much of a man for rules. A bit later his friend came 'round.

" 'I knew when I smelled that foul tobacco of yours that I had to live,' were his friend's first words.

" '*Mon pauvre vieux,*' said Dr. Pascal, 'You'd almost got me off smoking, but I didn't want to give you that pleasure . . . .' "

Monsieur Mons sighed. "He was the best. All heart. It's a great shame he's gone."

"Where does he live now?"

"In Milans. That's in Drôme. About twenty kilometers from Montélimar. He bought an old house there and he's restoring this and that. Makes his own wine, too, though it's said to be undrinkable."

Monsieur Mons babbled on but Robert's attention had wandered. Dr. Pascal . . . could he be the *P.* of the notebook? It couldn't possibly be Dr. Perrin. He'd only been living in Nizier for six years.

When he went up to his room at last, he had made up his mind. He'd go to Milans the next day to visit Dr. Pascal. Perhaps he'd be able to find out something about Robert Macy.

Why couldn't he leave it alone now? After all, he knew that Robert Macy was dead. Dead and buried. Past history now . . . . But what about Eleonore? The name on the medallion? When he'd asked Cristine where she had got the chain, she had said she'd found it in her mother's jewelry box.

106

" 'I should rather have liked to be called Eleonore,' she confessed. 'It sounds so beautiful.' "

Cristine . . . .

If he got back early from his visit to Dr. Pascal he'd go and see her again.

++++++++++++++++++++++++++++++++++++++

chapter nine

Robert got out of bed and went to the window. It
was a clear morning, the sky an innocent blue. Branches
were lying scattered here and there, trees were uprooted,
the twisted roots sticking out through the black lumps of
earth; relics of yesterday's storm.

After breakfast, Robert walked to the village. The road
had already grown familiar; the gentle slope going down-
wards with its various bends, the ravine, not deep, but certainly dangerous. They'd flung Oncle Lucien down there.

Robert halted and stared down. He shivered. He could
imagine him lying there on that flat bit, arms and legs
spread out like a broken doll.

He walked on hastily and tried to force the horrible picture out of his mind by concentrating on the view: the valley, the mountains, and the villages clinging to their slopes, the patches of green—those were pine trees—and, higher still, the snow caps.

The storm had driven away the suffocating heat; the air was cool and he breathed it in deeply.

When he arrived at the square he went to Lucette's café. She was busy sweeping up splinters of glass. The chairs were stacked, their legs pointing stiffly upwards.

"I've brought back Oncle Lucien's clothes," Robert said.

"If you wait a moment, I'll bring you some coffee. Go and say hello to Oncle Lucien. He's behind the house in the yard." She nodded towards the kitchen.

Robert saw the burnt-out candles there from the previous evening. A blob of wax had stuck to the wooden tabletop.

Oncle Lucien was sitting in a cane chair. His bald head shone in the morning sun. As soon as he caught sight of Robert his face split open in an enormous smile. There was something so touchingly innocent about it that Robert had to laugh. He took a chair from the kitchen and went to sit beside him.

"Hello, Oncle Lucien," he said in Dutch, "You look much better than yesterday. That Monsieur Moustache was really bothering you then, wasn't he?"

The gaping smile which had seemed fixed for good beamed even more widely and Oncle Lucien's lips bubbled an incomprehensible sentence.

"I've brought back your clothes," Robert told him. "Thank you again for lending them to me."

Oncle Lucien whinnied happily and took his hand. Robert felt embarrassed, but he didn't take it away.

Oncle Lucien made a few high sounds and a moment later started gently pulling Robert's hair.

"I suppose you want to borrow some for your own head." Robert hardly dared move because he didn't know how Oncle Lucien would react.

"I see you two are already the best of friends," came Lucette's voice, to his relief. "Whenever he likes someone, he pulls their hair. Good, eh, Oncle Lucien?"

Lucette ruffled Robert's hair teasingly.

"You're jealous of these beautiful curls, of course. Well, so am I! Wait a moment, I'll just put your hat on, otherwise you'll get sunstroke. Not that it would make much difference, but still, I'd rather not have that. Here . . . ."

Maternally she pulled on his hat. Oncle Lucien went on smiling undisturbed under the broad brim.

"I'm just going to give Robert some coffee. But he'll be coming back, mind. Then you can pull his hair again."

"I'd rather you did that," commented Robert.

Lucette laughed.

"How's the cellar?" he asked when they were inside the café.

"Oh, the water drains away by itself," she answered unconcernedly. "In fact, the cellar's always damp."

They sat in front of the window and looked out over the square where some children were playing. Their bright voices rang out and were carried into the café on the morning air.

"What are your plans for today?" Lucette asked.

"To go for a trip around here."

"That's why you're a tourist. Are you going on your own?"

"Yes."

"How?"

"I'll hitch." He finished his coffee and stood up. "Thank you again, Lucette. See you."

"Au revoir, Robert."

He crossed the square and set off at a brisk pace. He reached the main road quickly. He stood there at the side and made the well-known sign with his thumb. Cars swished by. Lots of foreign number plates, heavily loaded luggage racks and trailers towed behind. After a quarter of an hour he was lucky. A truck slowed down and stopped. "Where to?" a voice called from the open window.

"Montélimar," Robert replied.

"Get in," the driver invited him, "I have to go that way anyway."

Dr. Pascal's house was situated some way outside Milans. Robert had stopped to ask the way in a greengrocer's in the village.

It was a hilly area; a friendly landscape with softly glowing colors, very different from the forbidding-looking rocks around Nizier. There was a lot of broom here, thick yellow bushes that were nearing their end now. Purple patches of lavender mixed with fields of sunflowers. He also saw maize and vineyards, though the grapes were still small.

He turned left at the fork as he'd been told to in Milans. In no time he spotted an old roof tucked away among the oak trees.

As he approached, the house came into view. Seventeenth-century, he guessed, and well restored.

A woman was sitting on a bench in the shade. She was wearing a simple cotton dress and was busily shelling beans. It made a peaceful scene.

"Are you looking for someone?" She had a warm voice.

"I've come to see Dr. Pascal."

"My husband's busy in the garden. I'll just go and get him for you. Have a seat." She showed him to a reclining chair and disappeared behind the house.

Robert had not expected Dr. Pascal to be married to such a young wife. From what Monsieur Mons had said, he had expected him to be way over seventy.

He soon heard footsteps and then the two of them appeared.

Dr. Pascal was smaller than he'd imagined. He was thin, very thin even, and was wearing a pair of dull-colored trousers with a sloppy striped shirt over them. He had a shock of gray hair that stuck out wildly in all directions. Yet it wasn't his unruly hair that was most striking, Robert thought, but his eyes: they were an unusual shade of blue and they gazed keenly at you.

Dr. Pascal put out his hand.

"My wife told me I had a visitor. I don't believe I know you, do I?"

He sat down in a garden chair, took out a pipe and began to scrape out the bowl with a sharp instrument.

Robert took a deep breath. "No, Doctor, you've never met me. I've got a strange story to tell you."

Dr. Pascal looked at him, amused.

"My dear boy, at my age, nothing surprises me anymore."

"Would you rather I went?" asked Madame Pascal.

"No, no. You can listen to it, too."

"Then it can't be so terrible," the doctor commented as he took out a packet of tobacco.

"Let's have it! First tell me, though, who you are."

He had dropped the formal *vous* form and Robert began to feel more at ease.

"I'm Robert Reuling, Doctor, and I'm from Holland. The Hague. My father is Dutch and my mother French."

"So that's why you don't break your tongue over our language. So far it still seems very respectable." His eyes were laughing. "Go on, my boy."

"My grandfather died a year ago. He lived in Paris and was a doctor like you. After he died, my mother and I cleared up his flat. I found this in one of the cupboards . . . ." Robert took the notebook out of his jacket pocket.

"It belonged to someone called Robert Macy."

"Robert Macy," Dr. Pascal muttered, shutting his eyes.

"Robert Macy ... that name has a familiar ring. Yes, of course! He was the lad they got at the end of the war at the same time as Lucien ...."

He turned to his wife. "You know, that uncle of Lucette's who isn't all there."

His wife nodded.

"Did he ... did he know Oncle Lucien?" asked Robert, surprised. "Then that's who the letter L. must be! You see, the letter L. appears in the book. There's very little written in it, in fact. Can you tell me anything about him?"

Dr. Pascal pulled at his pipe thoughtfully.

"It's all a long time ago, towards the end of the war. I can't give you the details, because I wasn't there myself. Macy had in some amazing way managed to escape from a concentration camp where his whole family had been murdered. He had stayed hidden for months and somehow managed to keep alive. Don't ask me how.

"He was in pretty poor shape when Lucien found him and brought him to Madame de Béfort's house. She took him in and looked after him. A very peculiar woman who saved a lot of people, but who wouldn't hear of a decoration when the war was over. I suspect because of Macy.

"She never forgave herself for not being able to deliver the boy alive at the end of the war. Just the same, it wasn't her fault at all. In fact, he owed his death to an *histoire d'amour,* a love story.

"When Macy recovered, he struck up an acquaintance with a girl who often used to come to the house. They both got it badly and took to meeting each other in secret in an empty pension. Madame de Béfort knew nothing about that. Robert Macy had gradually become so expert over the months at escaping that it hadn't taken him long to spot a way out through the château cellars.

"They got him one evening. Killed instantly. Lucien was thrown into the ravine. He survived, but that's about all."

"The girl . . . the woman whom Robert Macy loved," was she called Eleonore?"

"Eleonore? No . . ." The doctor shook his head.

"The name Eleonore keeps cropping up in the book. It's the only one that's written out in full."

"No, she was called Pauline."

"Pauline!" cried Robert. "Pauline Girauld!"

"Yes, indeed. Do you know her?"

"No, but she's just died."

"Ah . . . we didn't know that," the Pascals spoke together.

Then Robert told them how he had come to be in Nizier. How he had found the pension Belledonne after a week's searching and had told Monsieur Mons that Robert Macy was his uncle. He told them about his visit to Madame de Béfort and how she had shown him the door when he had said he was Robert Macy's nephew.

"You should never go to Madame de Béfort with a lie," the doctor told him. "She knew only too well that Robert Macy didn't have a family any longer."

"Madame Girauld had just died when I arrived in Nizier. She's in fact buried next to Robert Macy."

"I hope she's found at last what she was looking for.

She was an unhappy woman," Madame Pascal remarked quietly.

"Did you know her?"

"I painted her once, years ago."

Robert looked at her in surprise. "A woman under a blue parasol?"

"Yes."

"I've seen that painting." He told them now about Cristine, about her accident with the moped, and his visit to the Giraulds' house.

"What made you eventually work out that I must be P.?" asked the doctor when he had finished.

"Because of Monsieur Mons. We were talking yesterday evening. It couldn't have been Dr. Perrin because he hasn't been living very long in Nizier. He talked about you and that's why I decided to look you up. Now I've got the L. too. That's Lucien. I met him at Lucette's . . . ."

"Yes, the poor devil. Luckily, he has a good life with Lucette."

Robert toyed with the book. "A Monsieur M. is also mentioned. Have you any idea who that might be?"

Dr. Pascal puffed at his pipe.

"Monsieur M., you say? Let's see . . . . It can't be Monsieur Mons. He only came to Nizier after the war. Then there's Morel the butcher. Not him either, he came in the fifties. The Matin family, no, they've only been there the past ten years or so . . . ."

Dr. Pascal shook his head. "I don't think I can help you there."

Madame Pascal asked Robert if he'd like to stay to lunch, and Robert gratefully accepted.

While she was busy in the kitchen, the doctor showed him the garden and explained how he made wine.

"I'll let you try some later and I'll give you a couple of bottles for Madame de Béfort. Then you'll have a good excuse to go and call on her again," he said, smiling. The meal was a relaxed one. Robert felt completely at ease. He recognized something of his parents' relationship in the way Dr. Pascal and his wife behaved; in the way Madame Pascal sometimes made an ironical comment to her husband and his teasing, good-humored reaction.

Madame Pascal knew The Hague well and also knew a lot about The Hague School of Painters. Robert felt ashamed that he'd hardly heard of any of the names she mentioned. Just the same, she didn't make him feel embarrassed for his ignorance. She was entertaining and stimulating and made him decide firmly to go and visit the Mesdag Museum as soon as he was back.

The Hague . . . . It seemed so far away.

Marjo lived there. Beautiful, defiant Marjo. She was probably lying on the beach at the moment or making love with some boy. It left him cold. He found it difficult to imagine her any more. She seemed to have dissolved, wiped out by the events in Nizier.

After the meal, Madame Pascal showed him her studio; it was a large room filled with canvases with warm, sunny tints, just like the painting of Madame Girauld. The room smelled of canvas and paint. An unfinished landscape was still propped on an easel.

His eyes moved along the walls and stopped at a portrait of a child.

Cristine! He recognized the expression at once. Uncertain and longing for love. She was holding a doll in her arms, pressing it stiffly to her as if she was looking for support from the plastic toy.

"That's Cristine," Robert exclaimed.

"Yes," Madame Pascal agreed. "I did it about seven years ago. I've rarely known a child to be such a good model. You only had to talk to her and she'd sit still. She always had that doll with her. You said you'd met her. What is she like now?"

Robert looked at the girl's head.

"Not very different," he remarked thoughtfully. "She still looks like that."

Madame Pascal showed him a few canvases that she'd just finished and told him something about them. His attention was elsewhere.

"Can I buy it?" he asked suddenly.

"Cristine?" She understood him immediately.

"Yes."

He looked anxiously at her.

She shook her head. "No, that portrait isn't for sale."

"Really not?" He was disappointed. "I'll ... I'll pay a good price for it. I've still got some travelers' checks," he pleaded.

Madame Pascal smiled. "I've already told you it isn't for sale. But I'll give it to you as a present."

"You mean . . ." Robert stammered.

"Exactly what I said. I'll give it to you. I'm glad Cristine's fallen into good hands." She lifted the painting from the wall. It was light because it hadn't yet been framed.

"I'll just wrap it up for you."

Robert stumbled over his words as he thanked her.

"That's enough," Madame Pascal laughed. "Come on, let's go outside again."

It was almost five when he left. The afternoon had flown by. Just before he left, Dr. Pascal disappeared again down to the cellar and came back with a couple of bottles of wine. "For Madame de Béfort. Tell her I'll be coming to see her soon."

Together, they watched him go.

chapter ten

Robert did not get back to Nizier till late that evening.

A bus was parked in the village square. Lucette's terrace was packed with tourists: large broad men and women with hats and red faces.

He wanted to walk past the café, but he heard his name being called.

It was Lucette. She was holding a trayful of jingling glasses and she looked hot; there were drops of sweat on her upper lip.

"Cristine's been in," she told him hurriedly.

"How was she?"

"I'll tell you in a moment. I haven't the time now."

He quickly took the tray from her and went into the café where he started to wash the glasses.

"The worst'll be over in half an hour," Lucette said before she ran back to the terrace again where orders were being yelled.

"Five Cokes, twelve beers, seven tonics," she chanted, reading from her piece of paper.

"How was she?" he tried again as he ducked into the refrigerator to give her the bottles.

"She's going to Paris tomorrow."

"What???" Robert gaped at her, open-mouthed.

She nodded, pushed away a lock of hair and called to the terrace: "*Une minute, bitte.*"

She went off again.

He didn't have a chance to exchange words with her during the next half hour. Lucette was doing good business. Her busy hands poured, gave change, and took away empty glasses from the tables.

At last the group got up and drifted back into the bus.

"Poof, what a day!" Lucette flopped into a chair. "It's all been happening today. It started this morning when they came to put back the pane of glass that had been shattered in the storm. Then a crowd from one of those holiday clubs came and hung around for hours, almost wrecking the place because they all wanted to play pinball. A bus from Reims this afternoon and those Germans this evening. And the usual customers in between." She passed her hand wearily over her forehead.

"Tell me about Cristine," Robert pressed.

"She came past this morning on her moped. She was still limping quite badly. She didn't say much, just that she's leaving tomorrow."

"Why so soon? She told me she was going to stay for the whole holiday."

"I don't know. She looked upset, actually. Something was bothering her and the awful thing was that I had no time to ask her what it was. There were people walking in and out and children all over the place whom I had to keep an eye on. There was no chance to talk, and then she slipped away."

"Do the Giraulds have a telephone?"

Lucette nodded.

"May I call her?"

" 'Course. It's in the passage."

Robert dialed the number Lucette had given him.

"Cristine Trabut," came the answer a moment later.

"This is Robert. I've been away the whole day. I'm at Lucette's at the moment and she's told me you are going to Paris tomorrow."

"Yes." Cristine sounded very depressed.

"Why?"

"I don't know. My grandfather wants me to. We've even had a fight. I'm . . ." She faltered.

"A fight? What about?"

"Because I didn't want to go. I want to stay here the whole vacation. I've never had a row before with my grandfather. Not till now."

"So what's going to happen?"

"I have to leave anyway. It's so unfair. I'm going to an aunt I hardly know. He's arranged it all."

"But why?"

"That's just it. I don't know. It's all so strange and I'm frightened. I don't think he can get over my mother's death. He's behaving strangely. Sometimes he calls me Pauline. That was my mother's name, and ..." Cristine began to stammer again. "I'm really scared, Robert. It's ... I'm ..."

"Can I see you again before then?"

"The train leaves Grenoble tomorrow morning at eight o'clock."

"Damn," Robert muttered and frowned. "Give me your address then and I'll come and visit you."

"Really? Will you really?"

She sounded so full of hope that his stomach tightened.

"I'll hire a moped and come and pick you up. We'll tear around Paris together on it."

Cristine laughed.

"When?"

"As soon as possible. What's your address?"

"My aunt's name is ...."

She stopped suddenly. Robert heard another voice. Cristine was talking now to someone else.

"Robert, I ..." then a buzzing tone.

He held the receiver a moment longer in his hand and then replaced it.

"Everything all right?" Lucette asked.

"I don't know." He stayed in the middle of the café, deep in thought.

"She didn't say such a lot. Only that she has to go back to Paris tomorrow. I must be leaving, Lucette. See you." He took his bag and the wrapped-up portrait.

"Au revoir, Robert," Lucette called.

It was a good quarter of an hour's walk to the Giraulds'. He couldn't even explain why he was going there. He was convinced that it was her grandfather Cristine had been talking to before the connection had been broken. He'd heard a man's voice very clearly.

The iron gate was already shut. The house lay behind in darkness like a black blob.

What was he doing here? Did he hope to see Cristine again? He'd have to ring the bell if he wanted to do that, but all the lights were already off.

He stood there indecisively. A heavy silence hung everywhere, broken only by a cricket or an animal escaping in the undergrowth. He could just make out a couple of bushes next to the gate. He hid the bottles of wine and the painting under them. Then he climbed over the gate. It wasn't difficult as long as he watched out for the sharp points on top.

He dropped cautiously to the ground on the other side and, avoiding the gravel, stepped carefully over the grass. The shutters were closed. Which room was Cristine's? Would she already be asleep? He glanced upwards. It was dark and quiet everywhere, as if the house were uninhabited. Suddenly he thought he heard a noise, the slamming of a door somewhere inside those walls.

But it could also have been his imagination.

He pressed on, his hand feeling the rough stone.

At the back of the house he saw a stream of light. Cristine? His heart thudded as he walked carefully towards the light. The shutters had been closed carelessly. The room seemed to be a study or a library with its walls full of books.

He stood on tiptoe to get a better look and had a shock.

Monsieur Girauld was there behind the desk. Robert saw him only in profile. He looked old and exhausted. In front of him were a bottle and a half-filled glass. The old man took the glass and finished it in one gulp. Then he filled it up again.

Robert suddenly felt ashamed of being there. He had no right to be spying.

He was about to turn away when Monsieur Girauld stood up, leaning heavily on the desk. Robert was struck by the forlorn expression on his face. He'd hardly ever seen such despair.

Monsieur Girauld walked to the bookshelves, reached up for a leather-bound book, and brought it back to the desk. He took a key from the book and used it to open a drawer. Then he took something out.

Robert caught his breath. Blood surged through his temples. A pistol! It was a pistol! Monsieur Girauld laid it down in front of him and looked at it. It was small and black, a toy almost. Then he picked it up, turned it over and over in his hands and put it down again.

Robert wanted to shout, but he did nothing. He went on watching as if he were turned to stone, and he saw Monsieur Girauld play gloomily with the pistol, putting it down, picking it up, then holding it right out before him as if he wanted to shoot it there in the room. Once he even aimed the barrel at himself.

Robert's whole body began to tremble. What should he do? Was Monsieur Girauld going to commit suicide? Out of desperation over his daughter's death? After all, Cristine had said that she was frightened because her grandfather was acting so strangely.

Monsieur Girauld was still clutching the pistol. Then, suddenly, he put it back in the drawer, locked it, and filled his glass.

Robert's breath was coming in uneven gasps. His hands were ice cold and he had to be careful in case his teeth started to chatter. He pushed himself away from the window and pressed his forehead to the wall. After a few minutes he was himself again.

The light was still burning.

Eventually he plucked up the courage to look again. Monsieur Girauld was still in the same place, motionless and gloomy. At last, at long last, he stood up. He went back to the bookshelves and replaced the book. He took the bottle and glass, and the light went out.

The night hung heavy and silent around the house.

* * *

Robert couldn't sleep a wink. As the hours passed the whole situation seemed steadily to get clearer. Cristine's grandfather was going to commit suicide when Cristine was in Paris. That's why she was being sent away. The more he thought about it the more worried he felt. He must get hold of that pistol before it was too late. He had already tried to open the window after Monsieur Girauld had left, but it was shut tightly. A transparent wall of hard gleaming glass stood between him and the weapon.

He dozed off for a moment but then awoke again.

Cristine . . . she was scared. Had she somehow sensed what her grandfather was planning to do? Did she know about the pistol? She was probably asleep at the moment in that square house, in among the bleak walls of family portraits. He imagined her asleep, curled up in the sheets with that twist to her mouth as if she were about to burst into tears at any moment. Or did that look disappear when she was sleeping?

Robert put on the light and slid out of bed. The portrait was tightly wrapped up. He worked the string loose and unwrapped the brown paper. The picture of the girl's head moved him deeply, more deeply than he cared to admit. The way she clutched the doll, too.

He ran his finger carefully over the paint. It felt rough. Colors and canvas, both so wonderfully exposing her inner self.

"Don't be scared," he whispered to the portrait, "don't be scared."

He switched off the light again and felt his way back to bed. He had to go to Madame de Béfort the next day. Monsieur Mons had been waiting up again for him when he came home and had told him that her housekeeper had rung up.

"She asked for you, but I told her you'd gone out for the day. She's invited you to go there for a meal. You'll have to go tomorrow now. I didn't even know you knew Madame de Béfort," Monsieur Mons had said reproachfully.

"I've only met her once."

"Ah, *mon garçon,* I wish I was in your shoes. Nobody ever asked me out after seeing me only once! Cristine came to see you, too. *La vieille,* the old woman, almost frightened her off the premises."

Robert turned over. His thoughts circled around Cristine, then moved on to Madame de Béfort. He'd been amazed that she'd invited him, but felt pleased about it.

The time slowly ticked by. He got up about half past four and hid the portrait in the cupboard.

The stairs creaked as he went down. A stale, stuffy smell hit him from the café. The smell of the Monses, old and sour. He was glad to get outside.

It was still dark. There were some hazy patches raggedly hanging in the wide silent valley down below him. Only a faraway truck broke the peace. The morning walk did him good. A soft breeze blew through his hair. The morning seemed so free of care it was as if that desk drawer with a pistol in it had been a bad dream.

The path wound around cornfields and rough grassland

where modern houses had been planted, the so-called country cottages of townspeople, often with ostentatious wrought-iron balconies. They marred the landscape and clashed with the old, sometimes ruined walls that had been there for centuries.

A rabbit crossed the path and leisurely hopped down a side path. Robert walked on. His steady footsteps sounded reassuringly in the early morning. They gave away none of the tension that was consuming him inside.

It was about five o'clock and beginning to get light when he stood before the iron gate for the second time. He climbed quickly over and crept along the grass. The shutters were still closed. He reached the back of the house, keeping close to the wall and being careful not to make a noise.

There were some outhouses there that had probably been stables at one time. One of the big wooden doors stood half-open.

Robert slipped inside. He saw a car, a gray Peugeot. He couldn't hide here, they'd find him immediately. He spotted a ladder in the half-light. When he climbed up he found himself in a kind of attic with some planks in it, broken furniture, iron bars, and reels of rope. The floor was a bit rotten and he had to be careful where he put his feet. He felt for a safe place and stretched out on the wooden planks. Everything was covered in a thick layer of dust.

He suddenly felt dead tired. What was he doing here anyway? What business was it of his that a pistol was lying in a desk drawer in the house? If Monsieur Girauld wanted to put a bullet through his head that was up to him. His business.

But I know what's going on, Robert thought. I know something about it all. If anything were to happen, would I share the responsibility because I hadn't interfered? He asked himself, Were you also guilty if you simply observed and didn't reach out your hands to help?

The darkness outside lifted but the mist before his eyes grew heavier. He gave in to an uneasy slumber.

He was startled awake by a noise that he was not able to recognize immediately. Then his surroundings crowded in on him. He was lying in the attic of an old stable and someone was opening the door below him. Light streamed inside.

He peered through the chinks in the floorboards. A rather young man was fumbling with the doorlock of the Peugeot. A moment later came the sound of the engine and the car was driven outside. He could hear voices. Robert slid forward.

Through a filthy window he could just make out a suitcase being loaded into the trunk.

There was Cristine. She looked even smaller and thinner than ever. Her grandfather was standing beside her, looking impassive.

The housekeeper was rushing backwards and forwards. Cristine shook her hand like a good girl and got into the car. Her grandfather got in in front, next to the driver.

"I'll open the gates," the housekeeper called out and hurried off.

Robert started to move. He had to be in the house before the woman came back.

He climbed down the ladder just in time to see the Peugeot disappear around the bend. Then he ran to 'the kitchen. The door was open. He stopped to think for a minute. The study was at the back, to the right of the kitchen.

He opened a door leading off the passage. Wrong. The next one then. Wrong again. He succeeded with the third. He recognized the oak bookshelves, the desk . . . .

First he quickly opened the window a little so that he could escape through it later.

Now for the book with the key. Was it in the fourth or the fifth row from the top? There were complete collections of Stendhal, Balzac, Anatole France, as well as Proust, André Maurois and Mauriac, all bound in leather.

His hands trembled as he touched the spines. For heaven's sake, which book was it? He didn't have much time. Monsieur Girauld was rather tall and, as far as he could remember, he had had to stretch up the night before. Then it had to be the Stendhal row.

He took a book out at random from the row. Nothing. His heart began to thump and his mouth grew dry. Then the next. That wasn't it either.

A door slammed. The housekeeper, of course. In his nervousness, Robert let a book slip out of his hands. He froze. Had she heard him? He waited tensely with bowed head.

He could feel his heart thumping through his T-shirt.

Nothing happened, and as he breathed out with relief, he suddenly spotted it. The books were tightly packed, their spines forming a straight line as if they were never taken out to be read. But there were a couple farther along which had been pushed in a bit too far. He took one out quickly. He was right! It was the fourth row! His feeling of triumph drained away as he heard footsteps in the passage. What if she came in? There was nowhere he could escape to now. If the door opened he'd be caught fair and square. He'd be accused of breaking in! To his enormous relief the footsteps went past the door and up the stairs. It was quiet again.

Now the drawer . . . his hand was shaking so much that it was difficult to get the key in the lock. It clicked and the drawer slid open.

There was the pistol, small and hard, like an innocent toy. He grabbed it and put it in his pocket. Drawer shut, key back in the book.

It was only now that he read the title. *"Mémoires d'un touriste"* . . . very ironic. Stendhal, he thought, I'll never in my life forget that!

He heard the footsteps again. He ducked to the window, pushed the shutters wide open, and jumped.

Panting, he pressed against the wall and wiped the sweat from his forehead. All stayed quiet in the room, so he quickly shut the window and pushed the shutters closed again.

The gate was still open. Once he was outside he ran and ran to put distance between himself and the house. At last, he went off onto a side path and sank to the ground. He pressed his burning face into the grass, then took the pistol from his pocket and threw it away from him.

He slowly grew calmer. He turned onto his back. The sky was blue with only a few fluffy clouds in it.

His watch said half past seven. In half an hour's time Cristine would be sitting in the train. Cristine in a compartment next to the window. Would she think of him?

"Will you really?" she'd asked yesterday evening when he had said he'd visit her. "Will you really?"

Suddenly he realized he had not even got her address.

++

chapter eleven

He got up after a while, picked up the pistol, and put it in his pocket. He felt very depressed. What he'd done was pointless. If Monsieur Girauld really wanted to do away with himself he still could. It would be easy to buy a new gun.

On the other hand, losing a pistol might make him stop and think. Who knows—perhaps he'd see it as a sign of fate, frustrating his plans. Robert hoped so. He walked back to the village deep in thought and went to Madame de Béfort's old château.

The housekeeper opened the door.

"Monsieur Mons gave me your message about the invitation to lunch," Robert said. "I'd love to come."

"Madame de Béfort will be expecting you about half past twelve," the housekeeper replied.

Then he walked slowly back to the pension where he went up to his room and hid the pistol in the bottom of his bag. He lay down on the bed and fell into an uneasy sleep.

He woke up just before half past eleven. He washed and changed into clean clothes and left with the bottles of wine that Dr. Pascal had given him. Madame de Béfort was waiting for him in the same room he had seen her in the time before.

Robert felt rather nervous. She looked at him coolly.

"I'm very glad you invited me, Madame. But first I want to apologize," he spoke haltingly.

"Oh?"

"I didn't tell you the truth."

"Please sit down." She waved him to a chair, but made no other attempt to make it easier for him.

"Robert Macy was not my uncle. The only thing we have in common is our Christian name."

"How did you come across his name?"

"In this notebook." He pulled the notebook out.

"I found it a year ago in a drawer at my grandfather's. He had just died and my mother and I were clearing out his flat.

"There's very little in the notebook but enough, just the

135

same, to have kept me busy for a year. I didn't know anything about Robert Macy and I decided to look for him. I followed his trail to Nizier. Unfortunately, I now know that he's been dead for some time."

Madame de Béfort took the notebook. She looked at it for a long time but didn't open it.

"Why did you pass yourself off as his nephew?"

Robert took a deep breath. "That just seemed to happen, Madame. For a week I'd been looking for a pension called the Belledonne. At last I found it. I badly wanted to stay there so I told them my uncle had been there before. Monsieur Mons repeated my story to various people, so then I couldn't go back on it. It would have sounded very implausible if I'd suddenly come up with another story. I'd much rather have told you the truth but you had a visitor and . . ." he faltered again.

"I wasn't completely myself the day you came," Madame de Béfort interrupted. "Hearing Robert Macy's name again took me aback, particularly coming from a total stranger."

"I'm really very sorry, Madame. Now that I've heard what happened to him I can understand only too well how you must have felt."

"What do you know about him?"

"That you were hiding him here. And that he was shot by the Germans at the end of the war."

"Who told you that?"

"Dr. Pascal. That's where I was yesterday. He gave me these bottles of wine to bring to you and asked me to tell you that he'll be coming to see you soon."

The woman's face opposite him softened and she smiled.

"Dr. Pascal is an old friend. I shall look forward to his visit. Let's go and eat. Then we can talk some more."

During the meal Robert told her about his conversation with Dr. Pascal. Madame de Béfort listened attentively, nodding every now and again.

"There's still one thing I don't understand," Robert remarked when he had finished. "How did my grandfather come to have the notebook?"

"What did your grandfather do?"

"He was a doctor."

"In Paris?"

"Yes, Madame. He lived there all his life."

Madame de Béfort smiled rather sadly. "Your grandfather found this notebook at the end of the war, not far from where Robert Macy was killed."

Robert stared at her in amazement.

"Did you know my grandfather then?"

"No. I met him only once."

Madame de Béfort was silent for a moment.

"It was at Lucien's. After that fatal evening .... Robert Macy's death still upsets me even after all these years. Not only the senselessness and cruelty of it, but why it had to happen.

"As you know, Lucien found him in the beginning. We made a hiding place for him in one of my cellars. Dr. Pascal could look after him only for a short while because then he had to go into hiding too. There was a price on his head, in fact.

"Robert's health improved visibly every day. He had an enormous will to live. His whole family had been murdered and he was the only one who had managed to escape. He almost felt he had a duty to live, a duty to his parents, his brother and his whole family . . ."

"Who knew that he was here with you?"

"Hardly anyone. Lucien, of course, but he was completely trustworthy. He was in the resistance just like Monsieur Girauld. Then there was Dr. Pascal."

"What about Eleonore? Who was Eleonore?"

"Ah, Eleonore . . ." Madame de Béfort sighed. "I haven't heard that name for years . . . . Once, when he was still on the run, Robert had found a chain with a round medallion with that name engraved on it. He gave it to Pauline Girauld, the girl he met here and whom he loved, just as she loved him.

"I can still remember what he said when he gave it to her: 'It's all I have.'

"He used to make her paper roses, too. Foolish things, but in wartime it's precisely those silly things that are so precious and stay in your memory afterwards. I can still see them: yellow paper roses that he would pin on her dress or put in her hair.

" 'When the war's over, I'll give you one every day,' he promised, 'a real one.' "

"Eleonore was the only name he wrote out in full," Robert said. "I noticed that she was buried next to him."

Madame de Béfort nodded. "Yes. They're both dead now."

Robert thought of Cristine.

"Did she . . . did she love him a lot?" he asked.

"Very much, I think. She was young and innocent at the time. War and the violence of war didn't touch her. Even Robert rarely spoke of what he had gone through. By that time only the present existed for him and she was that present. I doubt that she ever realized the danger to him of their secret meetings in the Belledonne.

"He was shot one evening on the way to the Belledonne. We only found him the following morning."

Madame de Béfort's expression grew sadder.

"At the ravine?" Robert asked gently.

"No. In the pension, in room sixteen. She was with him."

"But how . . . how did he get there?"

"I'll never know the whole story. She was waiting for him that evening and heard shots. She went to see what had happened and found him at the side of the road opposite the ravine. She didn't know then that Lucien was lying down at the bottom.

"Lucien must have put up a struggle; there were clear signs of that. It's difficult to understand why Robert Macy was such an easy prey for the Germans. A deadly shot, right in the center of his forehead. A man who had often escaped and knew everything about danger . . . ."

Madame de Béfort shook her head doubtfully.

"There was also a bullet with the notebook, Madame. Might that be the bullet that killed him?"

"No, it must be the one your grandfather took out of

Lucien's leg. He'd been shot too, but it was the fall down the ravine that completely damaged his brain."

Madame de Béfort was silent for a long time before going on. "I only found out about it all the next morning. I had got up and gone to the cellar to wake Robert. That was what we'd agreed. I wanted first to be sure that it was safe for him to come up. His hiding place was empty. I searched through all the rooms and then went into the village. There I heard that they'd found Lucien in the ravine just outside Nizier. He was still alive, but his condition was serious. There was a doctor with him.

"That's how I met your grandfather, who was passing through. Then we went together to the ravine. There was nothing to be seen. But a bit farther along your grandfather bent down and picked up something. This notebook. It must have slipped out of Robert's pocket.

"Then we noticed a trail, long dragging marks leading to the Belledonne. That's where we found them both. Pauline had pulled him there and stayed by him the whole night . . ."

Madame de Béfort's voice broke. "Robert had been dead for hours," she continued with difficulty, "and Pauline was completely distraught. We buried him quietly that evening.

"Pauline wasn't with us any longer. Her father had come home later in the day and taken her away with him. He was often away because he was in the resistance. He was horrified to hear what had happened. He tried everything to get her over her grief, but it didn't help much.

"I've often thought that the man who killed Robert Macy claimed another victim too, Pauline. She changed considerably and retreated more and more into herself." Madame de Béfort stared into space, seeing nothing.

"She never talked about him again. We grew apart after the war. She was often away on her travels, and when she came to Nizier, she would avoid this house. She married late, and had a daughter whom, as I've heard, you've met."

"Yes, Madame, but she's a long way away now. She's left for Paris."

They went on eating in silence. "Why did my grandfather keep the notebook?" asked Robert after a while.

"I wanted him to," Madame de Béfort admitted quietly. "I'd read the first sentence, which imprinted itself on my mind. *'I'm alive. God, how can this be true . . .'* It was too painful for me."

The housekeeper came to serve dessert.

"Des oeufs à neige. I hope you like that." Madame de Béfort still sounded upset.

"About thirty years ago Robert Macy sat where you are, eating the same dessert, which he liked so much," she said, watching him thoughtfully.

"Have some more, have some more," she pushed the bowl towards him.

"It's delicious, but you're not eating, Madame."

"At my age one's appetite grows less."

Robert looked at her. "Madame de Béfort is completely to be trusted," Robert Macy had written. He could easily see that.

"I'm very grateful to you for telling me all this," he said.

"It's a sad story, I'm afraid."

"Yes."

Suddenly a thought struck him. "There's a Monsieur M. in the book, too. Do you know who that could be?"

Madame de Béfort was sunk in thought and he had to repeat the question.

"Monsieur M.?" She shook her head slowly. "No, I don't think he knew a Monsieur M. Probably someone he'd met before."

"Yes, possibly. Oh, no, it couldn't be that." Robert picked up the notebook and flicked through it. "Look, here's *'Met Monsieur M.'*"

"Ah . . ." Madame de Béfort shook her head gently and smiled. "Perhaps he means Monsieur Moustache."

"Monsieur Moustache? Who's that?" His own voice sounded strange.

"It was Lucien's nickname for Monsieur Girauld. He had a moustache in those days which he'd kept on purpose when he joined the resistance.

" 'If they ever come after me they'll be looking for someone with a moustache. I'll shave it off then and nobody will recognize me,' he said.

"Lucien admired him enormously and had made up his mind to grow a moustache too when the war was over. He survived the liberation but was no longer fully conscious, poor man."

"Yes, I know. I've seen him," Robert muttered. He saw the image of Oncle Lucien in the cellar, screaming, his arms lashing through the air, his face twisted with fear. 'Monsieur Moustache. Bang, bang, dead . . . .' "

A dull, heavy feeling crept through him.

"Perhaps he meant Monsieur Girauld," Madame de Béfort suggested once more.

"Yes, perhaps," Robert answered.

With every step he took the name pounded in his head. Monsieur Moustache . . . that was Monsieur Girauld. He couldn't forget those few words in the notebook: "Monsieur M. hates me."

When he had said goodbye to Madame de Béfort he had asked whether she'd like to have the notebook, but she'd shaken her head.

"I won't be alive much longer. You keep it as your grandfather did. You know its history now."

Robert Macy . . . . Extraordinary that this man had played such a large role in the life of Cristine's mother without Cristine knowing a thing about it. Her mother had been living with a shadow all these years, the shadow of a dead man. He thought about Cristine's despair a few days back. She had also suffered from the death of Robert Macy.

Robert was approaching the ravine. Cristine had skidded

not far from here. He halted, walked to the edge and stared down into it. Then he looked around. He noticed a path at the other side of the road, narrow and overgrown. Might the Germans have been waiting there for Robert Macy?

A bullet in the center of his forehead. Instant death. Had they just picked on a passerby? How could they have known that he was in hiding? Had someone betrayed him?

He walked on slowly, lost in thought. The pension soon came into sight. Monsieur Mons was busy serving customers. Robert quickly went to his room. He wanted to be alone now and not have to talk to anyone.

Upstairs in the passage he stopped in front of room sixteen.

Here, Robert Macy and Pauline had met secretly and had then spent a night here after Robert had died . . . .

Monsieur Mons knew nothing of this story. He'd spun his own story around Madame Girauld. To him, she was the woman with the yellow rose who had come now and again to enjoy the view. He believed that she'd come because he didn't judge her as the other villagers did. He had no idea of the real truth.

Room sixteen. Robert tried to open the door, but it was locked.

Monsieur Mons must have done that. It was Madame Girauld's room. He stayed there for a moment. Pauline Girauld had spent a night behind that door with a dead man. *Eleonore . . . all that he had . . . .*

Her pain and despair must have been terrible as she held the lifeless body in her arms. She had loved Robert Macy deeply, Madame de Béfort had said. That same night she, Eleonore, had died too. A little each hour. Since then she'd refused to go on living. Robert came back to himself and went into his room. He went to the cupboard for the duffel bag. The pistol was lying there among his clothes.

He took it out and examined it closely. It was French. He had no idea whether it was loaded.

He carefully removed the magazine, a magazine for five bullets.

There were still three in it.

They lay gleaming and harmless in the palm of his hand. They looked so small and innocuous. The blood suddenly pounded in his temples. The three bullets seemed to be the same calibre as the bullet he'd found with the notebook.

He got up and looked in his jacket breast pocket. His hand was trembling.

He was right! They were the same size . . . .

It could be coincidence, of course. There must be hundreds of pistols the same size as this. Thousands, even.

Nevertheless, his heart thudded and his throat went dry. He could hear Cristine again: "I'm frightened, Robert. My grandfather doesn't seem to be able to get over my mother's death. He calls me Pauline sometimes . . . ."

He went over to the window. From here he could hear the holiday-makers on the terrace below, their bustle and laughter.

Inside him he could still hear Cristine's voice. Oncle Lucien's scream in the cellar, too.

He put his hands over his ears, but the voices didn't stop.

++

chapter twelve

It was late afternoon by the time he reached Grenoble. He left the bus at the town center. It was filled with terraced cafés and parasols under which brown-faced holiday-makers were gaily chatting.

Robert hurried through the narrow streets and asked a passer-by where he could find a shop selling guns. The man looked at him suspiciously, but gave him detailed directions as to where he should go. Left, then straight on, then, and then . . . . He had to ask twice more before he found the shop at last.

Hunting rifles, revolvers, pistols . . . .

The shop door was locked. A card on the door instructed him to ring the bell.

"Are you closed?" Robert asked the man who shuffled to the door.

"Oh, no. We keep the place closed as a precaution," he explained. He turned the key again once Robert was inside.

"I haven't come to buy anything," Robert said straight-away. "I just wanted some information."

He laid one of the cartridges on the counter with the original bullet next to it. "Are they the same?" he asked.

"It depends how you look at it," the man answered. "They're both 6.35 millimeters, but one has been fired and the other has not."

"Might they have been shot from this?" Robert took out the pistol.

"Hey, do you always walk around with that?" the man asked, taking it from him. He removed the magazine expertly and said, shrugging, "It's possible, of course, but it doesn't necessarily follow. It might just as easily have come from another pistol."

Robert considered. "Did the Germans use pistols like this in the war?"

"The Germans?" The man raised his eyebrows so high that Robert thought for a moment they were going to disappear under his hair.

"The Germans? Well, it's easy to see that you didn't live through the war. Do you really think Hitler would have sent his soldiers into war with a toy like this? Come, come, my boy! The Germans used Lugers. Look, here's one."

He went to a cabinet, slid the glass aside and took out a pistol. "Look, this is much heavier. Feel it. It's also much more accurate at long distances, and the bullets are 9 millimeters."

Robert held the weapon in his hand. It was indeed much heavier.

"If I shot anyone with this from a meter away would the bullet lodge in his head?"

"It would pass right through it," the man said. "Not this little one though. This isn't so powerful, though it is powerful enough to help someone kick the bucket. It's all a question of aim, of course."

"Would a small pistol like this never have been used in the war?"

"Everything that could shoot was used in the war. I kept a pistol like this for quite a time in my pocket when I was in the underground because it was handy and inconspicuous. Nowadays I sell them to women. To chase away men who are bothering them, see?"

Robert nodded.

"Why do you want to know all this?"

"A . . . a friend of mine has to write a story for a paper. A war story, but he hasn't a clue about guns. One of the editorial people had this pistol. He said he'd used it in the war. My friend thought it would have been a bit small, so I offered to find out for him."

The man laughed. "What a story that would have made if he let the Germans fire with toy guns like these! Tell him to come here himself. I'll be glad to talk to him about the war."

"I'll tell him," Robert said, sticking the pistol back in his pocket. "Thanks for your help."

A moment later he was back on the street. The traffic rushed by. He walked to the center and looked for a place to sit on one of the café terraces.

He resembled the other holiday-makers. A tourist in France, relaxed and free. He asked the waiter for a Coke. He took a long time over it. Not one of the talking, laughing people around him knew what he was carrying around with him. The pistol was hidden away in his pocket next to the notebook with the words, "I'm alive, I'm alive . . . ."

Robert Macy. A dead man he'd never known but in whose past he'd become entangled . . . a past that was not yet over.

He paid and then slowly wandered through Grenoble, but the squares with their old gray houses held no interest for him. At last he came to a park where children were playing. He sat down on a bench.

Fragments of conversation flashed through his mind. A lot that she could not understand, Madame de Béfort had said.

Robert Macy was a man who knew all about danger. Why hadn't he escaped the Germans that evening instead of walking straight into them? Why hadn't he at least put up a struggle like Oncle Lucien? Oncle Lucien . . . that scream in the cellar.

He tried again to go over everything that had happened

in Nizier since his arrival. Madame Girauld's, Cristine's mother's funeral. Her wish to be buried beside Robert Macy.

The afternoon he had turned up as Robert Macy's nephew . . . . Monsieur Girauld's bad turn when he heard the name. Then Cristine's hasty departure. Why? And now the pistol.

He guessed that Monsieur Girauld had been going to use it to commit suicide out of desperation over his daughter's death. The pistol, Monsieur Moustache's gun . . . . Robert buried his head in his hands. What was he to do? Robert Macy was dead. Murdered one evening during the war. The affair was over and done with.

But he knew more. He had a notebook with some words written in it that only he understood. "Monsieur M. hates me." Why did he hate Robert Macy?

He got up suddenly. He knew what he ought to do. Go and ask for Cristine's address in Paris. He'd tell Monsieur Girauld that he wanted to look her up. He had promised Cristine that. But would Cristine's grandfather permit a friendship between his granddaughter and a nephew of Robert Macy, whom he had hated?

The address . . . . What would happen if Monsieur Girauld refused to give it to him? He didn't want to think about that, or, rather, he didn't dare to.

He had come so far. He couldn't go back now. He had been wandering around for hours and hours, the tension building up inside him. He'd carefully worked out in advance what he was going to say, but the longer he waited on the doorstep the emptier his head became, until he hardly knew anything anymore except that he had to see this through to the bitter end.

He heard footsteps approaching in the passage. He stayed still, almost paralyzed with fear. He had never been so frightened. Frightened and alone.

The housekeeper opened the door.

"May I speak to Monsieur Girauld?" he heard his own voice ask. It was as if someone else were speaking.

"Monsieur Girauld does not wish to be disturbed."

"I *have* to ask him something. About Cristine," he persevered.

"Couldn't it wait till tomorrow?"

"No, I'm leaving then."

The housekeeper looked at him suspiciously, but then turned and went back along the passage. He stayed at the door waiting.

A little later Monsieur Girauld appeared, leaning heavily on his stick. "Come in."

It sounded more like a command than an invitation.

Robert's stomach lurched. He wanted more than anything else in the world to turn tail and run into the night. Run and run until he dropped. Instead, he followed the tall man with the stick to the study. This was where he'd been that morning. There was the desk with its now empty third drawer. There were the bookshelves with Stendhal's "*Mémoires d'un touriste*," with the key in it. And there opposite him was Monsieur Moustache.

"I understand you wanted to ask me something." His voice was cold and distant. He didn't offer Robert a chair, so he had to stand.

He looked at the man behind the desk. He seemed old and worn-out, with deep lines in his face and sunken eyes. Robert swallowed. "Yes. I'd . . . I'd like Cristine's address in Paris, please."

"Oh?" The gaze directed at him was devoid of all warmth.

"I rang her up last night, but the connection was broken. I intend to go and see her."

"Do you, indeed?" Monsieur Girauld spoke sarcastically. "Then I'm afraid that you'll have to forget that idea because I don't intend to give you her address."

He had refused! He had refused! The blood rushed to Robert's head and he found it difficult to swallow.

"Why not?" he asked hoarsely.

"Since her mother's death I have felt responsible for my granddaughter. I do not approve of a stranger visiting her."

"I'm not a stranger. I'm her friend," Robert broke in. "Was that why you sent her away?"

"That is none of your business." Monsieur Girauld was cutting. "As far as I am concerned, this conversation is over."

The implication was clear. Robert was to leave.

"But I'm her friend. I . . . I promised," he started again.

Monsieur Girauld stood up. "I have nothing more to say to you."

152

Robert summoned up all his courage. "Is that because of Robert Macy?"

The words were out. The face of the man opposite him did not change, but Robert noticed his body stiffen.

"Robert Macy?"

"Yes, the man who's buried next to your daughter." Robert kept his eyes fixed firmly on Monsieur Girauld.

"What has that to do with this?"

Robert's mouth was bone dry. The room was beginning to turn.

"You hated him, didn't you?"

There was a silence, a silence so heavy and oppressive that it drummed in his ears. He heard Monsieur Girauld speak from far away. "What are you trying to tell me? What do you want?"

"The truth."

Robert found it difficult to utter the word.

"The truth," he repeated. "Robert Macy was murdered."

Monsieur Girauld straightened. "Your uncle fell into the hands of the Germans. That is common knowledge."

"The Germans!" jeered Robert. "The Germans!" He couldn't keep himself under control any more, and his voice sounded as if it were someone else's. The words came tumbling out, words about a murder committed thirty years ago.

"It wasn't the Germans who did it. It was you! It was you who waited for him on the path by the ravine and killed him with one shot. One shot in the middle of his forehead. Robert Macy would never have walked straight into the enemy, but he would go to someone he knew, and that someone was you, even though he was already aware that you hated him. He never thought, though, that you would be capable of murder."

Monsieur Girauld gripped the desk tightly. "Do you realize what you are accusing me of?"

"Yes, because Robert Macy left something behind that you didn't know about: a notebook, with some comments written in it."

Monsieur Girauld's face froze for a moment, but then he quickly recovered, and said sarcastically: "And does it also say somewhere in there that·I killed him?"

Robert flushed. "The notebook isn't all there is. There's also Lucien."

"Lucien! *Mon pauvre garçon* . . . ."

"Yes, mad Lucien. He shouts your name when he's frightened. The name you had in the war, Monsieur Moustache!"

Monsieur Girauld leaned forward, his eyes narrowing.

"And there's something else. Something else, Monsieur Moustache . . ." Robert started to tremble.

"There's something else . . . the bullet, the bullet from Lucien's leg."

"The bullet?" whispered Monsieur Girauld.

"Yes, the bullet. The bullet fired from your gun, which I took from your drawer this morning. The key is in *'Mémoires d'un touriste'.*"

Something strange was happening to Monsieur Girauld's

face. His left cheek contracted till it almost looked as if it was paralyzed in a wink. An absurd, frightening wink.

He rushed over to the bookshelves, took out the book and returned to the desk. He seemed to have forgotten Robert's presence. He fumbled in fitting the key to the lock. The drawer slid open. Empty . . . .

Monsieur Girauld struggled for breath. Then he stared at Robert with eyes filled with a bottomless hatred.

Robert was terrified. Monsieur Girauld's face was twisted, almost unrecognizably contorted. His cheek was still jerking. You could see the hatred possessing him.

"*Juif! Juif!* Little Jew!" he spat out.

Robert shrank back and banged against a chair. That was it. Robert Macy had been a Jew, a Jewish refugee.

"How dare you? Did you ever think that I would let you lay a finger on Cristine? Just like that uncle of yours, that Jew. That intruder! How dared he, how dared he . . . ? Pauline, my everything, degrading herself with a Jew!"

Trembling, Robert listened. The man just a few meters away was beside himself with unrestrained hatred. He was spitting out the words.

"Yes, I killed that uncle of yours and I'd do it again. Every time he as much as looked at her, caressed her with his eyes, I imagined myself killing him. Pauline, Pauline, my own daughter. How could she? I waited for him that evening. They say that Jews are clever. He wasn't! He walked right up to me when I shouted to him. I shot . . . ."

Monsieur Girauld stretched out his arm in Robert's direction.

"But what about Lucien?" Robert stammered. "Lucien."

"That imbecile! He happened to be nearby and he recognized my voice. He wanted to run for help. Help for that Jew! I had no choice. Now Macy has Lucien on his conscience, too."

Monsieur Girauld suddenly returned to his senses. The mad hatred that had possessed him the moment before had been spent. Robert didn't know which was worse: the man full of blind loathing scarcely conscious of the words he was flinging out, or this old tottering figure groping for his chair.

Robert felt sick, utterly sick. His stomach lurched and he tried desperately to swallow. With difficulty he finally said: "Robert Macy was not my uncle."

Monsieur Girauld was staring into space. The words didn't penetrate. His gaze was completely empty.

"Petit juif!" he only mumbled.

Robert ran. He stumbled, scrambled to his feet again and ran blindly on. His breath was coming in short gasps, his own wheezing frightening him. At last he stopped. The evening was fresh, but it didn't cool him off. He was burning and glowing all over. He had fled from the Girauld house. This time he hadn't seen the housekeeper, but had let himself out. The only thing he wanted was to get outside, to get outside, away from that man. Then he had started to run. He didn't even know where he was, this area was new to him. A side turning, a dark path somewhere outside Nizier.

He dropped spreadeagled into a shallow ditch.

"*Juif!*"

He was haunted by the words that still beat through his body. Those eyes filled with inhuman hatred pursued him. He had never thought about this possibility of Monsieur Girauld killing a man because he was a Jew. A Jew who loved and was loved by his daughter.

Something snapped inside him. Tears streamed down his cheeks. Tears for Robert Macy, whom he had never known, tears for Cristine's mother and for Cristine, too. Cristine .... He would probably never see her again. He couldn't after what had happened this evening.

Robert buried his head in his hands. He was overwhelmed by a deep loneliness. The night grew black around him.

++

chapter thirteen

Monsieur Mons sat down heavily at the table. "Your last breakfast, *mon garçon,*" he said. "Eat as much as you can, you need it."

He leaned forward confidingly and winked. "You need it, though what you get up to every night is a mystery to me. You look all done in; I can tell you that. There's a girl behind this. You've only got to look at your face to see what's going on. White as a sheet you are, with circles under your eyes that have nothing good to say. Ah, *mon garçon,* if I were in your shoes, I'd do the same. What's she like?"

Robert smiled weakly.

"You're not telling, eh? You're right, *mon garçon*. I wouldn't either. Only trouble comes from that. She's obviously worth it though. Enjoy it. Enjoy it while you can. I can't say that often enough. Make sure you know which way the land lies before you get married."

Monsieur Mons glanced shiftily towards the kitchen. "Make sure you know which way the land lies. That's the voice of experience."

"I won't forget," Robert mumbled.

Monsieur Mons pushed back his chair. He looked at Robert, his childlike gaze suddenly shy. "Will you come back?" he asked. "I mean, next year maybe, or if not, the year after. You know, even though you don't say much I have the feeling you understand me.

"Madame Girauld is dead. She didn't say much anyway, just like you, but she always came back. That's why . . . ." Monsieur Mons pulled out his handkerchief and wiped his neck fussily. "That's why . . ." he repeated. "It isn't the same, of course, but I mean, you see . . . you have to have something to look forward to, don't you?"

Robert was moved, possibly because of all that had happened the previous night, but more likely because of the faltering admission of friendship the fat man across the table had just made. Monsieur Mons was a lonely person, happy for anyone to listen to him.

"As soon as I come back to this part of the world, I'll come and see you," he promised warmly.

Monsieur Mons's face lit up. "Ah, *mon garçon,* agreed. I'll keep you to your word. The room upstairs is yours. Room fourteen. Nobody else shall have it. That room's reserved, I'll say, for my friend from Holland. Nobody will set a foot inside it. More coffee? Let me pour you some . . . ."

After breakfast Robert gathered his belongings together and put them all into the duffel bag. He put the pistol in his pocket. Then he said goodbye to the Monses. He set off down the gentle slope to the village. The morning was clear and fresh and a soft summer breeze was blowing. The mountains stood out in sharp relief. His footsteps were regular, but as he approached the ravine they slowed.

At the ravine he stopped. He put the bag with the wrapped-up portrait of Cristine on the ground. He looked down at the rocks below. Rough, gray stone with some flat spots at the bottom.

He started to climb down carefully. His feet sought support, his hands gripped the rocks firmly. His progress was slow. At last he reached the bottom and stopped. Was this where Oncle Lucien had fallen? Innocent, wide-grinning Oncle Lucien?

He took out the pistol and looked at it for the last time. In the night, tossing in bed, he'd made a decision that nobody should ever know the truth, the terrible truth. Least of all Cristine. Everything had to stay hidden from her. It would ruin her life if she were ever to find out.

Cristine . . . a clear image of her arose in his mind: unsure and afraid, that tight twist to her mouth.

He found a crack in the rocks. He let go of the pistol and heard it fall way below. He climbed up again with a feeling of relief, took the bag and portrait, and continued on his way.

His footsteps were regular once more: one-two, one-two. Suddenly he stopped dead in the middle of the road. He shut his eyes. What had he just done? Whatever had he done? Monsieur Girauld was a murderer. *A war criminal.*

It was only now that he fully realized that fact. The man had committed murder, but could now walk around quite normally, free. He had been living freely for about thirty years. A murderer, who had killed someone in blind hatred and perhaps might do so again. Monsieur Girauld had said that himself in the insane moments when he was barely conscious of what he was saying.

What had he done! The one piece of evidence that he had held in his hands a few minutes ago was gone . . . .

Robert opened his eyes again. The broad valley lay before him with its powerful, majestic mountains facing him, their peaks covered in snow. The air was pure, the sky blue. But even as he watched, the landscape seemed to snarl, the mountains contract, and everything around him lose its freshness and shine.

There were clusters of people in the square talking excitedly.

Lucette's terrace was already filling up.

Robert recognized tall, thin Mademoiselle Dreu. She kept putting her hand to her mouth as if she didn't want to hear her own words.

"Berthe found him," he heard her say.

Robert walked towards the terrace. The minute Lucette caught sight of him she pulled him inside the café with her.

"The old man's dead. Old Girauld."

"Cristine's grandfather?"

The blood drained from his face.

"It was an accident. The housekeeper found him this morning. Apparently you were with him yesterday evening."

"Yes, I was," Robert stuttered, "but what happened?"

Before Lucette could answer, he heard his name being called from the terrace. It was Monsieur Grolot.

"Hey, you, Dutchman! Come over here. Have you heard? Monsieur Girauld is dead. Died in the night. Berthe says you visited him yesterday evening. How was he then?"

"He was alive," Robert found it difficult to bring out the words. "He was alive. God, how can this be true . . . ?"

The words from the notebook! He passed his hand over his forehead. He felt ill.

"You're as white as a sheet," someone said. "Here, take a drink."

A glass with something green in it was pushed at him. He took a big gulp. It tasted of anise.

"You look very out of sorts," Monsieur Grolot remarked.

"Was he acting normally?" a man with a gray moustache asked.

It was Monsieur Corneille.

"Normally?" Robert repeated foggily. "I don't know."

"Didn't anything strike you as strange?"

"No. Yes, rather. He looked tired," he gabbled.

"Tired? Nothing more?"

Robert shook his head. "But . . . but what happened?"

"Nobody knows all the details. After you'd left he wanted to read for a while. That's what he told Berthe, you know, the housekeeper. He stayed in his study and Berthe went to bed. She sleeps at the other side of the house and she's asleep as soon as she hits the pillow. A bomb could fall and she wouldn't wake up. She got up this morning and knocked at his bedroom door. No answer. She went on knocking and in the end opened the door. The bed hadn't been slept in. Then she went downstairs and found him . . . ."

"How? . . . How did she find him?"

"He had fallen forwards on the floor and was lying in a pool of blood with a gun beside him. She thinks he wanted to clean his daughter's gun. Though it's a strange time to start a job like that. They always used to go hunting together, the two of them. Or rather, she'd do the shooting while he watched. He couldn't even kill a sparrow and he had no understanding for guns. As you see . . . ."

Robert took two more gulps.

"It's easy to see what a shock it must be for you. Why did you go there anyway?"

"To get an address."

"But nothing struck you as strange?" Monsieur Grolot pursued.

"No," Robert faltered, "no . . . . Why?"

Monsieur Grolot looked around the circle.

"Why? Oh, just why. It was only a question."

Monsieur Corneille twiddled the end of his moustache.

"Even if he had been able to answer," he remarked, "it would still have made no difference. The man is dead," he added in English.

"Leave off speaking Russian," snapped Mademoiselle Dreu at him. "What's wrong with your own language?"

But Monsieur Corneille didn't even hear her. "The man is dead," he repeated solemnly.

Robert stood up. His head was bursting and the terrace was beginning to sway. He went into the café. His bag was still standing there with the wrapped portrait of Cristine beside it.

"Are you leaving?" Lucette asked, looking at him expectantly.

He shook his head. "I'm staying," he said tonelessly.

"Cristine will need you," she remarked. "I shall too, in fact. Here you go."

She pushed a trayful of glasses into his hands, and Robert began washing them.

About the Author

"Belledonne exists and was a source of inspiration," says Dutch author Anke de Vries. She is "fascinated by the French way of life," and though she lives in the Netherlands with her French husband and their three children, they often spend the summer in France. The author was born in the Netherlands in 1936, and spent a part of her childhood living under the German Occupation of World War II.

Ms. de Vries has written three other novels and a play in six parts for Dutch television. She also has contributed numerous articles to children's magazines.

DATE DUE
